I0700168

Kelp Journal

Issue No. 10

Editor-In-Chief David M. Olsen

Masthead

Editor-In-Chief
David M. Olsen

Managing Editor
A.M. Larks

Fiction Editor
Leanne Phillips

Poetry Editor
Maria Duarte

Non-Fiction Editor
Cymelle Edwards

Copy Editor
Chih Wang

Table of Contents

More than a Kerosene Lamp

by Christine Arroyo

I f you'd been dating this guy for six months, falling in love over shared environmental projects—his the ocean, yours the forest—if you'd been sailing down the Baja California coast for months, if you'd gone swimming with stingrays miles from shore, if he'd taught you how to dive for sea kelp, how to understand the migratory patterns of whales, how to identify wind and current details, if you'd fallen in love with his awe of the natural world, his commitment to veganism, then you, too, would be shocked when he brought out a kerosene lamp on the last day of the sailing trip, as if he knew that you'd take issue with it, as if he knew that you, who had handcuffed yourself to pipelines, spent nights in jail and only gotten off on a technicality, you who hadn't flown in an airplane or driven a gas-guzzling car for years, that you of all people would be especially offended by this kerosene lamp, that you would want to smash it and throw all the parts into the trash, that you, too, would feel a boiling anger inside of you as he swings the lamp like he's Ishmael from *Moby-Dick*, as you stand there wondering if you even know this man at all as he defends this kerosene lamp, saying how much he loves it, which makes you wonder if he loves it more than you, so as sea lions bark like dogs somewhere on shore, you tell him that kerosene burns even dirtier than almost any other fossil fuel, that it releases carbon dioxide and carbon monoxide, that the initiatives in Africa to replace kerosene lamps and stoves with solar power are because the kerosene is poisoning people, giving them asthma and cancer, that kerosene lamps are like the gateway drug to all fossil fuels, and you will stare at him in shock as he says he doesn't care about the carbon footprint of "one measly lantern"—his words, not yours—before you accuse him of being a privileged white male, and instead of being swayed by your passion, he then doubles down on this carbon-emitting lantern, holding it close to him like it's his firstborn child as he points out that the Lycra spandex bathing suit you're wearing is actually plastic and that your bathing suit is contributing to the poisoning of seabirds and the scourge of microplastics in every body of water on the planet. You look at him, speechless, and then you say, "My bathing suit isn't made of Lycra," even though you know it is.

Christine Arroyo's work has been published in *X-R-A-Y Literary Magazine*, *Flash Fiction Magazine*, *Dark Recesses Press*, *Beyond Words*, *Burningword Literary Journal*, and *Variety Pack*, to name a few. Her work has been nominated for *Best of the Net* and is also included in the *Best Microfiction 2023* anthology. She has just completed her first novel about siblings navigating an increasingly warming world.

How to Rescue a Skate

By L. Danzis

I f I close my eyes, I see your dock stretching into the White Oak River. It's sunset, the last golden fingers of light reaching across the gentle waves. The spiky grass prickles the balls of your feet as you cross the yard to get to the dock. The mid-June day has finally cooled from its 80-something-degrees to a mild warmth punctuated by the occasional brackish breeze off the marsh. The conditions are optimal for a little evening fishing before going back inside to do a crossword before bed, or chip away at the novel you're supposed to be reading for book club.

I watch as you fix the lure onto the line and cast; the last flecks of sunlight catch the hooks like falling stars before they vanish into the dark water. This is the moment you like most—the waiting, the stillness. There are just the night sounds of the marsh—the water lapping against the posts of the dock, the rustle of the breeze through the live oaks and sedge grass, the occasional splash from a far-off bass, maybe even the call of a distant owl.

The scene plays out in my mind like a dream. There are skips and lapses, blanks I have to fill in, like the time my wife and I went to the movies and a snowstorm cut the power. When it came back, the sound returned but the picture was still gone, so we had to use our imaginations and context clues until the projection started back up. Maybe you reel in your line a few times before casting again; maybe you catch a few small fry for bait in the crab trap; maybe you try closer to or farther from the reeds. Maybe the hair on the back of your suntanned arms stands up as the breeze blows, and you tell yourself, *One last cast.*

Only this time, when you reel in your line after feeling the familiar tug, your excitement dims. It's no whopper that wriggles through the water toward the dock—no late-season trout, no red drum, no flounder—but a skate, probably *Raja eglanteria.* It looks like a southern stingray (*Dasyatis americana*), but it's got some key differences—most notably no stinger, but instead a thorny ridge down the middle of the wings and tail (hence its common name, "brier skate").

Shoot, I imagine you muttering in the same tone of mild annoyance that you use when I've stolen your spot on the Scrabble board or when you've found whiteflies in your tomatoes. But you sigh and get ready to haul it out of the water to unhook it and turn it loose.

But the skate doesn't come out of the water. You tug on your line, and it's then that you look back down and see that the skate—in its thrashing resistance—has tangled the line around a crab trap. I would've cut my line and left it, and I wonder why you didn't. Was the lure valuable or sentimental? Would you feel guilty for leaving a hook in the sound and a skate tangled in a trap? Or are you just a better person than I am, one who doesn't like seeing other living things in pain?

* * *

My teen years are another part where the film cuts out—but this time, I'm the one who cut it.

When I got my first iPad, around tenth grade, I had full access to Googling the questions I'd started asking myself, questions with no Google-able answers, but the first wonderings of someone not at home in their body or mind.

> *How do I know if I'm gay?*
> *Can I be straight with a crush on a girl friend?*
> *Do all gay people go to hell?*

My searches yielded personality quizzes and unhelpful self-help articles. Without answers from the internet and without any queer adults to ask for advice, I held my breath and jumped into experiments headfirst.

I don't know what you thought as you watched me break one box only to try and force myself into another. I'd realized that heterosexual femininity wasn't for me, but even you could see my attempts at masculinity weren't suiting me either. You realized long before I did, long before either of us had the vocabulary for "nonbinary" or "genderfluid," that I was somewhere in between—the skate that needs both fresh water and salt water to thrive.

But at the time, I perceived your attempts to tell me I could still be feminine as a lesbian as a rejection of my fledgling identity, so of course I didn't want to believe you when you tried to point out that my first girlfriend was isolating me from my other friends. I said I was grown (I wasn't) and that I knew myself well enough to make my own choices (I didn't), and that you were rejecting me (you weren't). But despite our screaming matches, my icy aloofness, my biting sarcasm, you still saw your child, your weird little girl hurting, and you reached out even when you knew you might get stung.

* * *

Last winter you wanted to make a mosaic.

I suggested the shape of a stingray. We epoxy-pour-painted over old coasters and leftover bathroom tiles, and once they dried, we took them out to the garage with a hammer and finally spread everything on the dining table to assemble our masterpiece.

"Why'd we make it so big?" I asked after the first hour of trying to fit the shards onto the cutout and, standing back, realized I'd only pieced together the tiniest sliver of a wing.

In the same predicament, you laughed and kept puzzling. "Think how cool it will look when it's done!"

That's how I feel about piecing things back together with you. I've tried to atone through actions—coming home when I can, asking questions about your interests, learning your recipes, trying to know *you* as a person instead of only "my mother." And still, sometimes that never feels like enough, like I'll always be piecing together this mosaic without ever seeing the end result.

* * *

I watch as you ask your neighbors to help you shove out your kayak, and you paddle into the water that stretches like an indigo sheet between the shores. Had the skate stopped thrashing when you arrived? Had it resigned itself to its fate? That paints you in a heroic light—the savior rescuing the helpless animal—but that's not what I picture. Driven by the stubborn instinct to survive, the skate keeps flailing. I watch you reach out; the kayak wobbles as you recoil from the whiplike tail before trying to tug the line free from the wires of the trap. Paradoxically each tug only traps the skate further. In trying to draw it closer, you only push it farther away.

When the line finally snaps, I wonder if you consider giving up. I wonder if you continue your rescue only out of a sense of obligation. You've come this far, and your neighbors are watching from your dock. Or I wonder if you're doing it for your teenage daughter, independent but trapped.

You reach out, bare-handed. The kayak tips as you lean in to get your hand close to the trap, close to the thrashing tail and spiny ridge, close to the hooks. I feel the back of the skate's wings under your hand—prickly, but also smooth and sleek and fragile as wet glass. You try to grab it, and it struggles harder, its wings flapping as if it can shoot out of the water like a seaplane. And as you grip it tighter, the lure's hook embeds itself in one of your callused fingers.

I wonder if your first instinct is panic, if you try to shake the skate free or pry the hook from your finger to leave it there. Instead you grit your teeth and guide the skate from the trap until at last it's free. It's still attached to your hand by the other hook, and you'll have to paddle back one-handed, and you'll have to get the hook out of your finger. But the skate is safe.

* * *

You sent me a picture of the mosaic when you finished it.

Aqua wings outlined in a ring of royal blue, a vibrant orange stripe to highlight the purple ridge, wide-set blue eyes, a shimmering silver tail. It hangs on your wall with its nose facing out toward the sound, ready to swim.

It's the most beautiful thing we've ever made.

* * *

When you get back to the dock, your neighbors hand you up from the kayak and help cut the skate free. Its lip is bloody, and it's none too happy to have been out of the water for this long, but you know it's time to turn it loose, to let it fend for itself.

"Alright," I imagine you saying as you gently drop it in the water. "Now make better choices."

Your neighbors probably laugh before telling you to go to urgent care to get the hook out of your finger. And the skate—taking a stunned moment to process everything that happened—darts fearlessly back into the dark water.

L. Danzis has a BA in Creative Writing from the University of North Carolina Asheville, where they help coordinate the Great Smokies Writing Program. They are also a certified Inward & Artward Creative Facilitator through the Asheville-based arts venue Story Parlor, designing courses on how collaborative tabletop roleplaying games can be used as catalysts for independent writing projects. When they aren't learning about marine biology (especially cephalopods), they procrastinate writing by hiking, playing RPGs, and pursuing the perfect gin and tonic.

She may be lying down but she may be very happy by Jody Gelb

Review by Maria Duarte

She May Be Lying Down but She May Be Very Happy by Jody Gelb is a micro-memoir about how a mother processes the fact that death is inevitable for the child she birthed with cerebral palsy but also about how events in one's life help develop the self into what they are meant to be. This book is not about death, but instead it is about a life lived, however difficult and painful.

This micro-memoir tells the story of Jody and her husband, Marek, and the struggles a family must go through with a disabled child, and at the same time, we experience the growth of Jody as a mother and as a person. Lueza, their first daughter, was born with cerebral palsy, and at the beginning, everything seems like a disaster, but as time goes by, Jody and Marek not only learn how to attend Lueza's needs but also to enjoy being her parents.

The vivid images, the honesty transmitted with each admittance of error and of effort make this micro-memoir very candid and real about what a life with a disabled child can look like.

The book engages the reader by peeling, like an onion, Jody's humanness not only as a mother but as a person that still dreams of being an actress. It reminds us that mothers are individuals as well. As a society we put mothers' needs in the back burner, since being a mother must be the number one priority. But as Jody reminds us, mothers were individuals before becoming mothers. It is important to remember that if a mother cannot keep their sanity, then how will she take care of their children?

This book ultimately is not about the loss of Lueza but of the beautiful life they created while Lueza lived. It is about the life they experience with her, and most importantly about the moments they shared, since they will never come back.

Maria Duarte is a poet and writer who received her MFA in Creative Writing from the University of California, Riverside—Palm Desert. She has published poems in *Verdad Magazine* from Long Beach City College and in the anthology *The Good Grief Journal: A Journey Toward Healing*. She is currently the poetry editor for *Kelp Journal.*

Family Portraits by the Sea

Clad in linen, my gleeful mother scoots across wet sand
and broken shells to feel the froth of water on veined legs.

Her granddaughter surges like a dolphin through
the cresting waves. She is the guide who led

her to this place. I sit in a beach chair on the ridge,
stave a broken umbrella in the sand against

wind and sun, hunch to last till hunger calls.
I listen as their voices rise and break like egrets fishing.

My mother listens to our voices rise and break like egrets
fishing
in the wind. The sun lasts, hunched as hunger calls.

Umbrella staves pierce like blowing sand. She
reads in her beach chair on the ridge where she led us.

She is our guide, clad in linen. I surge like a dolphin
through the cresting waves. My gleeful daughter

scoots across wet sand and broken shells, red
shovel in hand, to feel the froth of water on her legs.

Brief Taste of Heaven

The search is always the same.
Boots greet miles of dirt and roots,
dream of rest on a wide outcrop,

granite or limestone buffed by rain,
fissured by ice, ancient sea scoured.
Slice salami and cheese on a ledge

that resists age and suffering.
Lean back in a hollow–cool in high
summer, warm in the late autumn sun–

one heel hedged on a fin of raised stone.
Here on the Beaver River, for example,
at the head of a waterfall, a playground

of boulders to clamber over,
each with a new view of the churn,
the pines, the ripening woods and gray sky.

I coil gingerly into pigeon pose on a rock,
the slab indifferent to the press of my weight,
the ache of half-century muscles and joints.

Later, I float the currents of Henry James'
sentences, while the river, stealthy above,

fierce below, steals breath from birdsong,

mutes outrage and the pillage of the train
rattling to the refinery by the bay. We
are young even when our bones turn

brittle and bruises bloom on our skin.
The falls spray time on dimpled stone.
And the stone's perspective?

Cartwheels of light through mist,
hurried sky, another human
storm gathering straight line winds.

White Landscape

I run with microspikes for the ice
where the trail is steep and exposed,

alone except for the occasional dog walker
trudging in his thick boots and coat

as the morning sun spills over the ridge.
We are at home any hour in the whiteness

and shadow of bristly snow-tufted cedar
bare spindly oak, bent prairie grass.

A pileated woodpecker tocks at the trunk
of a dead sycamore until it hears me

and stills, its red crown startling
against white sky and white bark. Its fear

lays quiet as rocks in the creek under snow.
The city bulges and sags with a brightness

that hurts if you stare—an old man
on stained sheets in a hospital bed

shimmering in harsh light. He shouts
about rights, demands dinner and a smile

from the nurses forced to work overtime.
The dog walkers and I nod beneath fleece

when we pass, beards threaded with crystals.
We are not hardy, or strong,

nor exceptionally intelligent—though
it is easy to get drunk on that draft,

loosen the tongue like one accustomed
to others listening. Ease comes from ease,

the habit of spikes on the ice, warm boots
in the snow, a well-stocked wood stove

waiting at home. Truth is
we have what it takes to feel safe

Sedimentary

(I.M. EGC, 10/16/2020)

1.
Friends call across the ocean to tell us
you died, Ester Gagliano Candela,
in the converted garage beside

the shuttered stucco villa
where your mother bunkers
in her dementia. They say

that when she heard the news
two tears slipped through
before she turned to her TV.

Sea breeze rustles dry palm leaves
in your father's garden gone to seed.
You know precisely how earth lifts and buries.

2.
Thirty years ago, Ernesto, dapper
even in his garden clothes, gently
scolds the straining dogs as he

ushers us past cascades of oleander
and bougainvillea into the cool

shadows of your parent's home, a comfortless

Victorian couch, coffee on a bright tile tray.
Lines in a newspaper brought us together.
Do you remember, Ester? Lemon, fig

and medlar branches strain
for the light that pierces your window.
Pecked fruit drops to rot in the yard

outside our gap-toothed garden doors.
There we huddle two damp winters,
except on weekends when we climb

black metal stairs to the heated flat
where you and Guendalina monitor
your daughter's sullen adolescence.

Your friends, soon to be ours, enlighten
us to local curse, demand twisted
vowel sounds from our mouths:

Auminnini u bar a pigghiarini nu caffé.
Windows mist while the pasta boils
and when we laugh too long and loud,

fogging the view of Monte Pellegrino.
In your kitchen I learn to tease ink sacks

from cuttlefish, stuff them with tentacles

and breadcrumbs, set to simmer
in sauce the color of sky meets sea
when dark comes on. It is the year

they chunk the Berlin Wall, shifting
Italian plate tectonics we need
you, a geo-physicist, to explicate.

Ester, you extoll the wines of Alcamo,
a certain butcher's stuffed rolled veal,
ricotta fresh from Piano degli Albanesi.
Doyenne of friendship, you lay bare
how a meal evokes past and future
gatherings, flora, fauna, magma,

forces we ride and sometimes cultivate.
I see, though I am not there, a pair
stooping to collect samples at dawn

on the gray slopes of Etna, the inky
slopes of Stromboli. You ignore any hint
we perceive you as a couple. Remember

that eggplant evening in Guendalina's courtyard?
So many ways of taming bitterness—
tomato, salt, sugar, vinegar—

you tend grill, she flits from
the kitchen, and in between,
hot embers, tired smoke.

3.
One last conversation at your nephew's
wedding, surrounded by the friends
you gifted us. Worn and thin as your failing

hair, dressed in a white sweater, you
shrug off questions about cancer,
fatigue, your mother's erosion,

inevitable as the course of lava
Sicilian politics, the convulsions of a
prickly stubborn island you taught

us to call home. Lines
in a paper brought us together.
Time presses us into place.

David Tager lives in Columbia, MO. His poetry, fiction, creative non-fiction and translation have previously appeared in journals such as *The Crescent Review*, *The Kenyon Review*, *Manoa*, *Well-Versed* and *Tamaqua*.

Rowboat

by Barbara DeMarco-Barrett

The sky was black as Nina rowed past the Fun Zone. Fairy lights stretched over restaurant patios, and the Ferris wheel that had been there forever spun about, its rickety bench seats looking like they'd snap right off should a strong wind blow in off the ocean.

Nina liked being out on the water at night. By then most of the tourists, who had clotted the bay since sunrise with rented eight-person canopy-covered electric boats, retreated to their hotel rooms, burrowed in at a bayside bar, or rode the ferry to Balboa Island, where 4,300 residents and a few blocks of shops—ice cream and frozen-banana stands, restaurants, boutiques—packed its 0.02-square-mile radius, leaving the bay to the party boats and to her and her rowboat.

The night smelled salty and dank, which she liked, and the water was like glass. The boat had no running lights, which could garner a fine from the Coast Guard, if they wanted to get picky, but money was tight. Most of Nina's income from typing up medical reports went to paying back the money she'd embezzled, so on moonless nights like this, she was super vigilant lest she got run over by a yacht. Roland, her last boyfriend, had a vintage muscle car he sped around town in, but he refused to go boating. She could put her own life at risk, he said, but he wasn't about to get run over by a party boat.

Bridges and a ferry connected Newport Harbor's eight mostly residential islands. Out on the water, traversing the narrow canals, gliding beneath overpasses, Nina imagined what Venice felt like—not that she'd ever get to Italy. After she had served a year in CIW (California Institute for Women), she was lucky to return to Newport Beach, with its palm trees, surfers, and the book club she'd been a part of before she was sent away. In prison, reading was the only thing that had kept her sane.

She rowed toward Celine's house down by the harbor. Lovely book club member…that Celine. It had been two weeks since the last book club meeting, but the wound remained fresh. In front of everyone, Celine had made fun of her for being a convicted felon.

"You'd have to be a dunce to get caught embezzling," Celine had said. Everyone laughed, and one member, Jackie, who always hosted in her big oceanfront house, nervously changed the subject to her impending first Botox appointment and her worry that the treatment might freeze her forehead in a scowl instead of getting rid of it.

Nina couldn't forgive Celine. Nina's boss, Jimmy Toldano, made zillions by peddling knockoff jewelry and purses. If only he'd given her the raise she asked for, Nina wouldn't have had to embezzle it from him. What's worse, Celine had been a friend before prison, yet the year Nina was sent away, Celine was the one book club member who never visited, never wrote a letter, never even sent a book.

But that night two weeks ago Celine went on and on, joking that Nina was their first trailer-trash club member. Of course, she was kidding, of course! Yet the comment cut deep. Nina waited for Celine to apologize, but she never did, even though she could see how much it had affected Nina.

Nina had talked about her festering hurt feelings to her parole officer Jamie Lerner. "She never said she was sorry," Nina whined.

"Some people aren't good at sorry," Lerner said. "You need to find a way to deal with frustrations. They're a part of life."

"At night I go out on the water and row," Nina said.

"Rowing is a great exercise," Lerner said, "and a healthy way to deal with your frustrations, but is it wise to go at night? You could get run over by a party boat."

"I'm careful."

"It's that temper of yours that really concerns me," Lerner said. "Remember to always, *always* count to ten. Better yet, count in Spanish; it takes longer."

*   *   *

A three-story yacht blasting disco glided by, rocking her rowboat. Nina held onto the sides and looked into the inky water. If she fell in, she'd survive. The bay wasn't more than twenty feet at its deepest point and less than fifty feet from shore. You'd have to be an idiot to live by the bay and not know how to swim.

At the last book club meeting, Celine said she was taking swimming lessons, now that she lived beside water, but scoffed because she wasn't making progress: she hated getting wet. Brilliant.

As Nina reached Celine's bayside home inherited from her parents, she stopped rowing but drifted in the outgoing tide. Celine's house had floor-to-ceiling windows. At night, when the interior was lit up, it was like peering into a life-size diorama. Nina had rowed by the house many times, especially since the night Celine had been mean to her. The blinds were never drawn. Exhibitionists liked to be watched, and prowlers liked watching. Nina knew a few in CIW who would love all these curtainless bayside homes.

Tonight, Celine was with someone. A man. Nina raised the binoculars she kept in the boat because you never knew when there was something you needed to see up close, and saw Celine pour wine into the man's glass. Roland's glass. Roland? They toasted. Celine held her baby finger aloft. Didn't she know it was déclassé, raising your pinky when you consumed wine or tea? Nina wanted to bite it off and feed it to the fishes.

Nina had introduced Celine to Roland at the book club's holiday party right before she caught him cheating on her, which she learned through Instagram, of all things. The idiot had let his other squeeze take selfies, which the stupid girl posted.

Roland had a great kitchen where he'd made fresh pasta for Nina, and even madeleines, though he had a bad habit of spitting, and he had an eye tic that acted up when he was nervous. Nina had been willing to overlook his nerves and filthy habits, but she couldn't forgive his cheating. Yet now that Celine was with her old blinking, pacing, and spitting boyfriend, Nina was having second thoughts. What was up with that?

Lerner's voice was in her head. *Count to ten.* Uno, dos, tres…

* * *

Nina wasn't pining for the jerk; he'd served his purpose. She had met him at the Blue Beet bar soon after she was paroled, and he helped pass the time as she acclimated to life without bars. He was also good in bed. But he wanted some say in how she dressed and what lipstick she wore. Freak! He even wanted her to get a boob job. She had said she'd get a boob job if he got a penile implant, and he had the nerve to be insulted.

She felt like screaming, but out here on the bay, near the boardwalk where a few pedestrians strolled about, screaming wasn't a great idea. She breathed in the briny night air, reminded herself she was lucky to be back in Newport and not in her cement cubicle. She rowed home fast and screamed into her pillow.

The next night, Saturday, Nina went out on the boat again. The air smelled salty and moist and made her skin feel soft. She promised herself she wouldn't do it, but she couldn't help herself: she rowed to Celine's. And there they were, Roland and Celine, swilling wine from long-stemmed glasses, kissing and slobbering all over one another. *Close your damn curtains.* Nina had to do something.

Cuatro, cinco, seis…

Book club was coming up that weekend. She didn't want to go, but she had agreed to bring dessert.

She went to Target—Targét to her—to buy cupcakes. Rubicon cupcakes were the best, short of baking them yourself. She would bring a cupcake for each member to take home in their own miniature pink box with their names calligraphed with a black Sharpie. Yes, that would be perfect.

Nina found the laxative capsules she was looking for in the pharmacy aisle. She'd inject the powder into Celine's cupcake. The results would be harmless but annoying. Then, for some odd reason, she found herself on the pesticide aisle—kismet? Or was it that old song "Strychnine" by The Sonics roaming her brain. Rat poison. She'd inject only a smidge into the cupcake, just enough to make Celine sick but not kill her. She'd wait till just before book club to inject it lest it flavor the cupcake. And if at dinner Celine apologized for being so mean, then of course, she wouldn't do it at all.

The following Sunday night, the book club met on a member's patio to discuss *Anna Karenina*. Nina sat beside Celine, ready to give her every opportunity to apologize. Most of the women empathized with Anna and understood how distraught she must have felt after Vronsky's rejection, but not Celine.

"What a weak-kneed, lily-livered excuse for a human being. Get over it, Anna!" she said, making everyone laugh. Celine could be a stand-up if she'd wanted.

The group dined on a grape-and-cheese charcuterie, stuffed peppers, a green salad with pomegranate seeds that got stuck in your teeth, and wine—lots of wine. And cupcakes.

As the group on the patio enjoyed dessert and opened another bottle, Nina excused herself to use the restroom. Kramer, the resident border collie who had sat by her feet when she was eating, followed her inside. Instead of going to the bathroom, Nina headed for the pink boxes. Kramer must have known something was up because he kept dropping a red ball at her feet. Nina threw the ball and shuffled through the boxes until she found the cupcake box with Celine's name. She was about to inject it with rat poison when Kramer dropped the ball on her foot and whimpered. She looked into his eyes and seemed to catch the message he was sending: What if someone other than Celine ate the cupcake?

"Who *are* you?" she asked Kramer, and threw the ball in frustration.

* * *

The next night Nina got in her rowboat and rowed to the center of the bay. The air smelled of seaweed and salt, and the water was rough from a storm brewing and bucked the rowboat like a pony. Fifty yards out, a ferry heading for Balboa Island crossed with three cars and a flock of pedestrians. Might the wake be strong enough to capsize the boat? She wasn't worried about herself, because she knew how to swim.

Nina had invited Celine because she thought: captive audience! And to her surprise, Celine had accepted! Now Nina would make Celine understand how upset her comments had made her. Now she'd get these dark thoughts of revenge out of her mind. Celine was human, wasn't she? Somehow, Nina would make her understand and would make her say she was sorry.

The sky was a peachy pink as a dozen party boats loitered on the water. A few bloated yachts three and four stories high blasted disco and kicked up waves, rocking her tiny boat. She rowed to Celine's bayside home a quarter mile south, where she waited on the dock. Celine waved eagerly, and Nina threw her the line. Celine caught it and wrapped the line around a mooring buoy. Then she handed Nina a two-person cooler and tossed her a canvas bag crinkly with snacks. Finally, Celine stepped in, tipping the boat, making her gasp. Water sloshed over the gunwales. Celine was a big girl—top heavy, she liked to say about herself with a grin.

"I can't swim," Celine said, settling on the low bench.

"Don't worry," Nina said. "We won't be too far from shore, and it's not that deep. There's a life preserver under there." She pointed at the bench.

With the oar, Nina directed the boat close to the mooring and freed the line.

The sky was the color of a three-day-old bruise. The tide was coming in, making it harder to navigate the rowboat. From the top of the tote bag, Celine produced a candle.

"Vanilla." She set the small, metal votive on the bench beside her and lit it.

Fifty feet away, Fleetwood Mac blasted from the speakers of a Newport party yacht that jiggled the rowboat as it glided by. Celine held on. A fishy-smelling wind blew in.

Celine reached into the cooler and withdrew a bottle of wine and two stemmed wineglasses.

"Glass can be dangerous on a boat," Nina said.

"Would you rather I put them away? You know I like to live dangerously." Celine winked.

"No, it's all right, this time."

Celine always brought the best wine to book club.

The boat drifted.

Celine poured and they toasted, but instead of Nina feeling of good cheer, that image of Celine and Roland bloomed before her, and she felt steamed all over again.

"I've been thinking," Nina said, preparing to talk about how she'd been feeling and wanting to discuss the matter like mature human beings.

But Celine interrupted.

"What was it like in there?" she asked. "Do you miss anything about it?"

"Seriously?" Nina said.

"I bet there's something," Celine said in a singsong voice.

"Oh, yeah, I miss the food. Five-star dining every night. You'd love it." Nina's jaw hurt. Stress made her clench. She took up the oars and rowed toward the center of the bay.

* * *

"Should you be doing that?" Celine said, no longer singsongy. "That yacht is headed straight for us." She gulped the rest of her wine.

"You like to live dangerously, right?" Nina wore a devilish grin.

By now the yacht was maybe ten feet away, and the Lilliputian rowboat rocked wildly from the swells just as Celine stood up to wave at the partygoers. A swell jogged the boat sharply, and Celine toppled backward into the water. Her glass went flying and her mouth made an O, green eyes awestruck. Her back hit the bay. Nina could not believe her good fortune. Celine flapped her arms, trying to keep her face above the water. The partiers were oblivious to what was going on down below.

If I wanted to, I could push her head down with the oar.

Poor Celine flung her arms about like an octopus.

"Stop thrashing already," Nina yelled.

"Help me!"

The bay was cold, and Nina hated swimming at night. There was no telling what was in the dark water that might sting or take a bite. No way was she jumping in, and she didn't want to watch her drown after all, so she threw Celine the life preserver and, with great reluctance, pulled her to the boat.

"Put your hands here," Nina said, placing them on the sides. "Now try hefting yourself in." Celine's big boobs kept catching on the side, but finally she made it in. She looked so pitiful; her hair smooshed flat against her skull like a wet dog.

"I thought I was going to drown out there," she said, wringing the bay water from her hair. Her eyelids fluttered with recognition. "You *wanted* me to drown, didn't you?"

"Of course not," Nina said, halfheartedly.

Just then the *Tiki Boat*, a two-story party boat, glided past, the Allman Brothers' "Whipping Post" playing at top volume.

Nina gave Celine her jacket—her teeth were chattering. A party boat passing the other way blasted "YMCA" with the partiers dancing, making letter shapes with their arms.

As the rowboat aimed for the Fun Zone, the ferry crossed in front of them, and someone who looked just like Roland leaned on the railing with a woman in pink. The way his arm was around her, this was no relative.

"Oh my God," Celine said.

"What?"

Celine pointed. "The bastard. We have a date for later. He said he was working till ten."

"You used to make fun of him when we were dating."

"I know I did, but then, shit, I fell for the asshole." Celine's eyes looked moist. She held a hand over her quivering mouth. "And he's really good in bed, too."

"Yes, I know," Nina said, dryly.

Celine shook her head. "I should kill the bastard."

"Men have died for less."

Celine pursed her lips. "You'll help me, right? You probably know how to get away with murder. Isn't that what they teach you in prison? How should we do it?"

"You can't be serious," Nina said.

"Serious as a heart attack," Celine said.

They rowed to Celine's mooring. Nina jumped out, roped the boat to the buoy, and Celine climbed onto the dock.

Nina said she'd be glad to help, but this time she'd make damn sure it went wrong. That would be apology enough.

Barbara DeMarco-Barrett is editor of, and contributor to, *Palm Springs Noir* (Akashic). Her stories are in *Coolest American Stories 2022, CrimeReads, USA Noir: Best of the Akashic Noir Series, Rock and a Hard Place,* and *The Dark City Crime and Mystery Magazine.* She received a Distinguished Instructors award from University of California, Irvine, and teaches at Gotham Writers Workshop and Saddleback College. *Pen on Fire* was a *Los Angeles Times* bestseller. She hosts the podcast *Writers on Writing.*

Interview with Edan Lepucki

By A.M. Larks

Edan Lepucki was gracious enough to chat with me over email—despite birthdays, illnesses, holidays, and other crazy scheduling during the month of November—about *Time's Mouth,* her latest novel as well as her many other published works. What resulted was a far-reaching conversation about human nature, the craft of writing, and unintentional genius.

[KELP JOURNAL] In *Time's Mouth,* place is a central feature, and it struck me that, like memory, places can be a portal; they can evoke specific times, eras, and events. For me, sleepy San Luis Obispo will always be the town I went to college in, and when I am there, I will always feel like the person I was. The places—settings in *Time's Mouth*—are no different. Characters often are transported (figuratively) back to who they were when experiencing a familiar place. Did you intend from the start to meditate on the transportive nature of place when writing *Time's Mouth*? And how did you approach such a broad subject?

[EDAN LEPUCKI] To be honest, and maybe this is giving me away as a sort of idiot when it comes to my own work, I didn't intend for place itself to feel like a portal to the past, or for the book to be a way to explore how strongly identity is tied to place. However, the more I write, and the more I have my stories and novels read by smart readers (i.e., not idiots like moi!), the more I realize how central setting is for me. I'm from and live in Los Angeles, and I'm basically obsessed with the mythologies of the state. I'm interested in how the daily experience of life in LA, and in California overall, interact with, confirm, and subvert these widely perceived notions and stories about it.

But on a more practical level, when I'm writing, I need specific, concrete, literal places for my characters to inhabit. In my writing class at Caltech, I'm fond of quoting Elizabeth Bowen's dictum, "Nothing can happen nowhere." That is, you can't place your characters in a vacuum and expect it to work. Setting allows for action to occur, and it also influences action, pushes it in intriguing, dramatic directions. Setting also gives you tools to play with as you move through a scene: trees to look at, birds to hear, walls to touch, and so on. That all takes on meaning, even as it also remains literal and practical. Like you, and like anyone, I suppose, places from my past do exert a kind of charge and hold a significance, allowing me to reflect on who I was, who I am. I guess I brought that feeling to the book.

[KJ] I think a lot of great writing is subconscious. And I was wondering if, like with your unintentional and brilliant use of setting as a portal, you have always meant to focus on other types of portals. In all of your novels, your characters are looking for a way to escape the present, whether that be the time-travel way of *Time's Mouth* or turning to alcohol and social media as in *Woman No. 17.* Even in 2050 apocalyptic *California,* drugs and alcohol are still utilized to transport the characters away from the harsh realities in front of them. Is this just something that humans do, long for a way to escape?

[EL] I didn't intend to create these other portals of escapism for my characters, though I agree with you that they're present in all of my books. I'm interested in getting character consciousness on the page, and when you do that, when you get into a fictional person's interiority, you're able to show a character spinning off into a fantasy world, into a place of longing for comfort, solace, and forgiveness. There are the organic thoughts anyone might go to, to create these pleasant feelings, and then there are the other tools people use to cope. We don't have time travel (or, I don't), but there is alcohol, drugs, social media. In my fiction, I'm interested in those tools because they're short-lived. The character must return to reality and must contend with how their expectations and desires aren't met, how they're upended. The end of the fantasy, the closing of the portal as it were: that's where the drama lies.

[KJ] And drama there is! Your novels all capture and describe the high tension and wildly dramatic moments in the lives of your characters, a sign of good art. Which brings to mind *Woman No. 17*, which discusses the perils and benefits of being the subject of art, specifically of a famous artist. It literally hangs over (or in the closet of) Lady. And I wondered if being the subject of a famous work can haunt your life, if the inverse is true for the creator of art. Do you think artists are haunted by their most well-known or popular works?

[EL] It seems to me that most artists are only obsessed with what they're currently working on. That's the case for me. Once I publish a book, it leaves me. It's strange: I spend so much time immersed in a world and its characters, and then, poof, it's published, and it's gone from my consciousness. I still retain affection for my past work, but I feel dread at the thought of going back into any of them. Honestly, whenever anyone mentions an older work of mine, I feel vaguely embarrassed! Don't get me wrong: of course I'm grateful to talk about any of my work, ever! It's just that a process of alienation has to occur to allow my most private obsession into the world. I have to let it go. I don't feel haunted by my most popular book—*California*—but I do think it's funny, in an anthropological way, that readers gravitate toward that one precisely because it was a bestseller. It's fascinating that people want to read the one that most others have read, even if it's the one that received the most mixed reviews. I prefer people to read whatever book I finished most recently, because I feel I'm getting better at my craft with every novel, and because the most recent one is the best representation of me, as an artist, right now. Perhaps artists who have a MEGAHIT feel haunted by that success. I have never suffered by such star power!

[KJ] I have heard many writers express the same sentiment, that they grow in their craft with each novel or book. But one bit of craft that was so impressive (and necessary) in the world of *California* was your descriptions. I was amazed at how you were able to describe the settings so in-depth without resorting to using the names of things. I could picture every detail; it all felt so familiar, and yet completely different. How did you approach this feat, the writing of a setting in a world that did not yet exist?

[**EL**] Thank you! I am so glad to hear it because, well, I love to describe stuff. It's probably my favorite part of the writing process: imagining deeply and trying to translate what I imagine onto the page. That's really all it is— imagining deeply, and from the perspective of the character whose POV I'm favoring. *California* takes place in the future, but it's not an unrecognizable one. It contains so many relics of our own present, and so it wasn't hard to propel myself there. For me, scene and plot can't emerge without concrete details, and so I spend time figuring out the specific and literal objects surrounding characters and imagine them interacting in these specific places to make the story unfold. My friend Darcy once gave me the incredible advice to "imagine even more" when I am in a writing rut. Sometimes our block is that we haven't gone more fully into the scene, into the particularities of the dramatic moment. If I lean in closer, look deeply, it gets clearer, has intention. That really helps.

[**KJ**] What fabulous advice. I am definitely going to lean into "the peculiarities of the dramatic moment" moving forward. Thinking of this type of intense focus, I was wondering if you could talk about the drafting of your novella *If You're Not Yet Like Me.* How was that similar or different from drafting your longer works?

[**EL**] I don't remember too much about writing *If You're Not Yet Like Me* except that the editor Deena Drewis asked me to write a novella and assured me it didn't have to be a "real" novella (whatever that is), simply a long story, as long as it has to be. That felt very freeing and took the pressure off. I also felt confident because, for the first time ever, I knew the manuscript would have a home, and I wouldn't have to face rejection upon rejection before it was (hopefully) published. That made me feel bold, and I wrote what I wanted, leaning into a fun, but sort of naughty voice. In the end, it was a novella in name only. It's only about thirty-five pages…a story! For me, stories and novels are themselves, formally speaking, before they're even drafted; I've never had one become the other. I enjoy short fiction for the brief investigations into a character or premise. The novels are entire worlds that I want to be immersed in for years.

[KJ] One of the things I love about *If You're Not Yet Like Me* is that the narrator tells the reader how to read her story. Passages like "Be careful, then. You will spend your life assuming things, Baby. About me, about the world. And you will often be wrong." Or "I can feel you getting excited about Zachary, and that excitement is dangerous, for this doesn't end how you want it to. This isn't a story of a woman who sheds her superficiality, who learns to love someone as they truly are, and in the process learns to love herself. It might have been that kind of story, had things gone the way of happily-ever-after, but they didn't. The ending changes everything that came before it." The premise of *If You're Not Yet Like Me,* of a mother writing to her unborn daughter about who her father is, allows for the breaking of the fourth wall, which is really fun. Do you think this is the kind of story that has to be in short form rather than a longer novel-length narrative?

[EL] The breaking of the fourth wall, the direct address, in the novella happened by accident. That is, in an early first draft, I had this incredibly forward, declarative narrator, and she was talking to the reader—to someone. I had to stop (after page two or so, very early) and decide, *Well, who is she speaking to?* That dictated what happened in the story, because when I had the idea of her voice, I didn't realize she was pregnant. Once I realized she was pregnant, it changed the entire story: what happens in it, what matters to her, how the narrator's perspective evolves. I had a similar situation with *Time's Mouth*, where I had this imperious narrator who was omniscient, and I wondered: *Who is this?* It ended up being the keeper of time itself! But, you're right, with a novel, such conceits feel like just that, a conceit if it interferes with the story and characters too much. So I had to pull back the narrator in *Time's Mouth* so that it began the story and was an organizing principle, a global intelligence, but not a central component. I am in awe of novelists who can pull off a major conceit, like the second person, for instance, which is easy in a story but very difficult in a novel, which, to me, has to be more immersive and deeper than any formal flourish.

Edan Lepucki was recently nominated for the Joyce Carol Oates Prize in literature for her most recent novel, *Time's Mouth*. She is also the author of the novella *If You're Not Yet Like Me* and the novels *California* and *Woman No. 17*. She is a graduate of Oberlin College and the University of Iowa Writers' Workshop, and her fiction and nonfiction have been published in *Esquire*, the *New York Times Magazine*, *The Los Angeles Times*, *The Cut*, *Romper*, and *McSweeney's*, among other publications. *The Los Angeles Times* named her a Face to Watch for 2014. She was the guest editor of *Best American Nonrequired Reading 2019*, and her story "People in Hell Want Ice Water" is available as an Audible Original.

A.M. Larks' writing has appeared in *NiftyLit, Scoundrel Time, Assay: A Journal of Nonfiction Studies, Five on the Fifth, Charge Magazine,* and the *Zyzzyva* and *Ploughshares* blogs. She has served as a judge for the Loud Krama Productions Emerging Female and Nonbinary Playwriting Award and has performed her stories at Lit Up at Town Hall Theatre in Lafayette, CA. She is the managing editor and blog editor at *Kelp Journal.* She is the former fiction editor at *Please See Me*, the former blog editor of *The Coachella Review*, as well as the former photography editor at *Kelp Journal.* A.M. Larks earned an MFA in Creative Writing from U.C. Riverside at Palm Desert, a JD, and a BA in English Literature.

Drunk Driving in Barbie City

Sara Marchant

My brother, Marvin, crucified my Ken doll upside down on the Dream House balcony when I was eight. He used so much tape and blue yarn securing Ken that I was forced to ask my eldest sister for help. Exhausted after working a twelve-hour graveyard shift at the hospital, she called our mother to see what Marvin had done. Mom stopped laughing long enough to say, "Marvin, we don't crucify people in this family."

When I tell this story now, it serves to judge whether I can be friends with a person. If you gasp in shock over Ken's crucifixion, we're probably not a match. Laughter before you share a similar Barbie horror story? You are my people. A third type of interlocutor will ask when I will put this scene into a novel, and the answer is most likely never. My family doesn't like it when I write about them.

As a child, when I complained about my brother's treatment of my one and only Ken, especially beloved due to his black hair instead of the usual blond, Mom reminded me that Marvin had wired one of his G.I. Joes' wrists together before dropping him down the chimney to slowly roast over our winter fire. The entire family agreed Ken had gotten off easy. Mom did make Marvin give me his surviving Joe, with his creepy felt beard and karate-action arm, to live among my Barbies and Ken, although Joe only came up to the others' shoulders.

"Height doesn't matter when you're horizontal," Mom muttered to my two adult sisters as I put Joe away in his new bed next to Skipper. I wouldn't understand this for many years.

Ken's clothes fit Joe if we—and by "we," I mean my niece Nancy, my contemporary with whom I shared a bedroom and the Barbie City we'd built after convincing our mothers to remove the bottom bed from our bunk—cuffed the arms and legs of the leisure suits, but he was never accepted by the Barbies. Even Ken, now duct-taped at the waist after Marvin put him on a homemade rack and pulled until the strong rubber band mechanism holding his two ends together snapped, held Joe in little regard. Joe understandably developed a drinking problem and took to joyriding the orange and pink Corvette. These drives always ended in tragedy. My niece and I started reenacting this storyline after my sister's inebriated ex-boyfriend drove his convertible under a semitruck and was decapitated.

Later on, when the Purple Pieman and his wife, Sour Grapes, who were the antagonists from the Strawberry Shortcake series, were given to me for my birthday, my Barbies had another man to choose from. Or share. They embraced the why-choose lifestyle before we had names for it. The Purple Pieman was elderly, shaped like a knobby villain, and *married*, but Barbie didn't care. He was male and smelled delicious. Years later, when white irises bloomed in the garden of the house I shared with my new husband, I inhaled the fragrance and sighed "Purple Pieman" in ecstasy.

In addition to the Dream House in Barbie City under the bunk bed, the slightly too-small Sunshine Family house inherited from my sisters, and the houses my niece and I made from cardboard boxes, we owned the Dream Recreational Vehicle, a banana-colored motorhome. Naturally, Joe lived there with whichever Barbie he was married to at the time. For a while, he was married to our twin Skippers until Marvin explained why that was flat-out wrong "on many levels, Sara!" After a divorce party, Joe married the off-brand pregnant "Barbie" that I'd convinced my mother's boyfriend to buy for me at the local book festival. Off-Brand Barbie and Joe moved into the trailer park while the Skipper twins moved back home with their grandmother Sour Grapes.

We were the type of children who found it normal for the apple pie–scented grandpa to live with his much younger mistress, so we weren't fazed that the Purple Pieman hadn't divorced Sour Grapes. Besides, it was too sad for grandparents to have a divorce party. I'm not sure why my niece and I were certain that adults had parties when they divorced? Maybe it was because Mom was so happy when hers was finalized that she took us out for ice cream.

Recently, when I asked my friend Kit-Bacon why she didn't allow her daughter to have Barbies growing up, she cited the unrealistic body expectations and all the pink. She gave her daughter that flat-footed, no-waist hippy doll, but her daughter turned out normal anyway. I wanted a hippy doll because she seemed like the right size for poor, stunted Joe with his overly muscular karate-chopping arms. Plus, their philosophical differences as a Vietnam vet and a dropout flower child would have made for excellent storylines.

But most of my Barbies were inherited from my sisters or given as birthday presents. I never saw the hippy doll until I was a teen, but I did finally have a doll that looked like me—dark eyes and hair and a rounder, more

Mesoamerican face—when Pacific Islander Miko debuted in 1985. With her popularity, more dark-haired Barbies became regularly available. In kindergarten I was excited to buy Black Peaches 'n Cream Barbie for my friend Tenisha because I wanted *someone* to have a Barbie that looked like them. Raised fifteen miles from the Mexican border, I knew only one blonde girl in our class until we reached the more populated middle school. Sometimes we called the blonde girl Barbie. She didn't like it.

When my middle sister's children were playing with Barbies, enough dark-haired versions were available that my sister's little blonds could pick and choose at the store. They also had what seemed an obscene amount of Kens compared to the man-doll desert my eldest niece and I had endured.

By this time of course, the Barbie City was long gone. My mother had remarried, we moved to San Diego, my stepfather had money—but I was too old for Barbies. The remnants of the city fit into one box "house" that I used as a traveling case when I went to babysit my sister's children. This box contained the twin Skippers, two dark-haired Barbies (Erzebet and Anemone Crowe, the love children of Russell), Crucified Ken, Amy Isabella Coverrubias, and the Purple Pieman with his no-longer-estranged wife. Joe had disappeared. (Marvin claimed innocence, but during his punk years, he'd shaved Astronaut Barbie's head and nailed her to his bedroom wall, so I have suspicions.)

Also in the box were a blue plastic sofa; an inflatable, hideously striped loveseat; vintage outfits galore; and the mesh shirt from the infamous gay Ken that Mattel released in 1993. He sported what appeared to be a cock-ring necklace that my sister had thrown out when her girls and I weren't looking. Once emptied, the traveling box became Barbie's studio apartment complete with trompe-l'oeil furniture, wallpaper, and windows. What stories this generation of nieces (and their little brother) and I enacted with these treasures! What narrative events we still talk about today!

By the time my sister's children were "too old" for Barbies (they tactfully overlooked that I was a grown adult), my eldest brother's daughter was the perfect age to play. Tragically, Sasha did not care for dolls of any kind. In vain, many times did I bring out the Barbie box, now residing in the home I shared with my husband. I introduced the narratives I'd developed years ago, told the backstories for each character, explained Purple Pieman's gloriously checkered past. Sasha had to admit he smelled delicious. Half Russian, she appreciated the dark and often disturbing history of the Barbies in the box. Had Amy Isabella Coverrubias really cut the brakes on the Corvette because she wanted to marry her sister's husband, Crucified Ken? She had.

Sasha was ten when she asked to take the box home with her to San Diego. "For a visit." Being uninterested until now, she had no Barbies of her own. Her mother helped her carry the large box containing multitudes to the car.

Two months later, during a family gathering, I suggested we bring out the box and play. Sasha, busy kicking around her clear, plastic hamster ball, looked stricken.

"Where are my Barbies?" I asked, filled with foreboding.

Her mother answered. Sasha hadn't played with them, and the big box was taking up much-needed closet space. My Barbie box had been given to a local Armenian daycare center.

My shock was overlooked by everyone because at that moment my husband realized Sasha's kickball held a living creature, and he raised justified hell. It wasn't until we left that I asked if they could get my Barbie box back. I'd only *lent* it to Sasha; it was a lifetime collection that spanned generations.

"You want I take toys away from refugee children?" my sister-in-law asked.

The entire family turned scandalized faces to me, and the subject was dropped, but I still don't see why I was in the wrong to ask. They were mine. I didn't give consent. I wanted them back.

You'd think I'd be invested in the new Barbie movie. I've been told by friends and family that I must be—and I'm sure I'll see it eventually. My friend Cassandra Lane, the only other adult I know who has as deep a relationship with her Barbies as I, wrote a glowing review of the film. But I'm really not interested in the movie. It's so pink, as Kit-Bacon would say. Margot Robbie is so blonde. Ryan Gosling looks like Ken's dad. I don't have a foot fetish, and Greta Gerwig's smug, twee style irritates me.

I was never in thrall to the mythology of Barbie. I didn't want to dress like her or wear the bright makeup or be an astronaut in a shiny, pink suit or change my outfit from Day to Night. I never felt maternal toward my Barbies or their siblings and children either. I gave the Heart family twin babies to my nephew Alex, who named the boy Ish-kibibble and loved him passionately until he was dropped in a Target parking lot and lost forever.

The Barbie box contained all the stories my nieces and I told ourselves to explain the world, and the family, we were born into. It's no coincidence that I started seriously writing after my Barbies were given away. A few years later, I was accepted into an MFA program, and after graduation, I published a novella and then a memoir. Does this mean all is forgiven for my lost Barbies? Or that I would have never written had I never lent out the box? Absolutely not. To both questions. But I'm still bitter.

Every time I walk pass the curio cabinet where my slowly growing new collection of Barbies is staged, or when I put together the Barbie Nativity after Thanksgiving (I'm a Jew), or if that earworm "Barbie Girl" song plays in the grocery store, I wonder where my Purple Pieman is living his sweet-scented life. Is he being appreciated? Is he getting the action to which he became accustomed after decades of play? We will never know.

My second eldest niece, now thirty-five and the mother of four, recently sent me a link to a Barbie-endorsed housewares line. She was very excited; her dream has always been a house like Barbie, and she expected me to feel the same. I didn't. Not really.

I never wanted to *be* Barbie. I didn't relate to her blonde perfection, the materialism, all the pink, plastic high heels. Playing Barbies for me was testing the boundaries of what our lives could be. What we are capable of, as well as reenacting the fluidity of the boundaries of the adults who were raising us. The twin Skippers and Crucified Ken and the Purple Pieman were tools, means to an end, and losing them taught me to use new ones. I'm grateful for what I've been given, please don't misunderstand. And that Barbie-themed pink-ombre area rug is pretty rad, my second eldest niece forced me to admit. We're waiting for it to go on sale.

For Christmas I gave my husband a G.I. Joe Navajo Code Talker doll. This Joe doesn't have a karate-action arm, but he does call for air support in Navajo when you press a button on his back. He lives with his wife, Navajo Barbie, and his girlfriend, Plains Nation Barbie, in the curio cabinet. The family has two plastic horses that belonged to my husband when he was a little boy. When Marvin comes to visit, we make sure the cabinet is locked. After all, I've learned my lesson.

Life's fantastic.

Sara Marchant received her master of fine arts from the University of California, Riverside at Palm Desert. She is the author of *The Driveway Has Two Sides*, published by Fairlight Books. Her memoir, *Proof of Loss*, was published by Otis Books. Her latest novel, *Becoming Delilah*, was published in August 2023, and her essay *Haunted* was a Notable Mention in Best American Essays and Nonfiction 2021. Sara is a founding editor of the literary magazine *Writers Resist*.

The Dreams of Birds

by Sam Moe

What happens last is I leave. I know, *I know* I always leave. What no one ever asks is whether or not I was given a choice. Could I have stayed, dealt with everyone, moved through my heart, whatever they're saying these days? Eat the circumstances and whatnot. Turned my feelings into fuel for nightmare poems and dreamy short stories.

For what it's worth, I was planning on staying. I would have gotten another cake, or even a bottle of wine from the cellar, if you'd let me. Jules is the one who didn't want to try anymore. And I know, I know I'm dramatic; she told all her friends I yelled at her in the parking lot (false; I yelled at *myself*, about myself, but I guess you were right about the parking lot). And then there's you, ocean gem, trusty pearl, lightning strike, always telling me you didn't want things to end this way, with food on the floor, unraveled yarn, no one eating your apple pie. I'm getting ahead of myself again. And what did I tell you about green-apple pie?

I got your text about the writing, and you're right. Always, always, I'm going to write about you. I have been writing about you, and I'm probably not going to stop. I'm not in love with you anymore. You got that part wrong.

* * *

What happens first is we go to the grocery store.

You're up ahead with my mother, arm in arm, checking out the pears for a potential galette. I'm back by the candy dispensers with Jules.

"Your mother sure is taking the grief process well," she says. She reaches into a dispenser filled with chocolate-covered banana chips, puts four in her mouth.

"She loves desperation. Don't buy into it, or she'll never leave you alone. She's even constructing a series of three-act plays about him." I lower my voice, so it's just my lips brushing up against her ear. Someone scowls at us, and I wonder if it's because we're married or because of the banana chips. "Don't take your medicine at the table, she's going to give you a lecture."

Jules laughs so loud and openmouthed, I can see stray chocolate clinging to the side of her tongue.

There are Christmas trees coated in rainbow lights, strings of greasy garland, shining ornaments in different shapes. A metallic reindeer, sunflower lit from within, bright red petunia. There is an orb with someone's name on it I don't recognize; then I remember we're at the supermarket, and it's probably the name of an expensive potato chip company or maybe even the manager.

Without giving it a second thought, I put the disk in my pocket. *Robin*, it says. If I could change my life, that would be the name I'd pick.

You walk over to us, your arms full of fruits. Golden Delicious apples, yellow as your favorite poison-frog patch at your old lake house. Northern Spies, Cortlands, something with the word *wolf* in its name. Peaches and bright pink rhubarb, a piecrust tube (to satiate my mother, I'm sure. I know you better than that), grapes the color of moth wings. Your fingers gripping mason jars so tightly that your skin becomes white as bone. Once, when we were at the lake house (even my mother, when my father was still alive), we got stuck in the mud. Not everyone, just you and me. Do you remember your duck boots? The same color as apples in October, orange like candy. You spilled your iced tea on my legs, and we laughed so hard and loud, a flock of birds revealed themselves from the trees, catapulted to the sky. You pulled me out of the mud, and I don't know why, but I told you your house was my home. Your lake house, not your real house. And do you remember what you said?

"Pretend you're having a nice time," Jules says, squeezing my arm.

"I love you, too," I reply, stuck in the murk of my own mind.

Jules frowns, kisses my neck.

You raise an eyebrow at us, asking if we can get in line already because your arms are *fucking killing* you.

The dream always starts the same. I wake in a field of golden light, all wheat and discarded hay bales, the tail of what I think is a cow waving in the wind, but I don't know, can't tell in all the sunshine. In the background is low chatter. In earlier dreams I thought it was my mother speaking to me. Now I'm older, and I've had the dream several times. Now I know it's you. You're on the phone, talking to me, but I can't hear what you're saying. I try to look for you, but the field is empty, aside from me (aside from the creature). I don't think twice about Jules. I try running in every direction; I always wake up before I reach the edge of the pasture.

All this is to say the gold of the field is the same gold as your grandmother's knit blanket, which is always folded in a neat square on your L couch. When we get home—

to your home, not ours—Jules abandons me to sleep on the couch. She doesn't ask whether she is allowed to use your grandmother's blanket. She doesn't take her shoes off or offer to help with dinner. She's been working all week, teaching graduate seminars about Harold Pinter and absurdism; her legs are tired from standing, and her arms are tired from writing on the board. We both have muscle issues, but my mother only knows about mine.

In the kitchen are photographs of mothers. Not your mother, not your partner's mother, but all the other mothers. Some I've met before, when we used to take sculpting classes together in the old mill, down the hall from the adopted cats, taught by a woman who only wore bad Christmas sweaters made by her daughter. Does a mother want a daughter? Or does she hope for something less menacing? A cherub or a goldfish. A ghost. If I asked my mother if she wanted me (and believe me, I've tried— on the lip of the tub, Sasha painting her toenails bright red; I'm ten and bleaching my eyebrows, fingers covered in bandages. I ask her if she still loves me, and she calls me ridiculous. She laughs. We both smile at each other in the mirror), she wouldn't have answered me. She hates all topics of discussion, including interpersonal relationships.

Other things my mother hates talking about are blackouts, alley cats, rats, and centipedes. She hates the fungus on the porch but enjoys when the neighbors have an aquatic breed of bees growing in the corner of their pool, loves our cat named Lulu but never wants to see another dog for the rest of her life. She likes riding the bus downtown but hates when a stranger sits next to her, prefers the window seat and always wants to die alone. Once when we were fighting—do you remember that day? The sky orange-purple, neither of us sure if looming was hurricane or tornado, you were in the living room labeling old photographs; we weren't dating, but we spent so much time together, my mother didn't know what to make of us—they found a body by the river. Deer at first, then rumored to be boy, hooves for hands, a scoop-necked T-shirt, a compass in his pocket, boy face, animal antlers. We went out with lanterns to help the locals drag the body from the edge of the lake. No one questioned who it was, or what. Soon the lights went out. We hurried him by the old well. You squeezed my hand and my mother smirked at me. She hates love, too.

"Who are all these mothers?" my mother asks.

"Women I know, people I've seen in the street. Back when I thought I would have an exhibition that mattered," you say.

"People came to your exhibition." I came to your exhibition.

You smile at me, and Jules smiles at the both of us, and I wonder if this was the moment of her witnessing.

Did she know, even then, about the incapability of letting go? She squeezes my hand. The oven chimes happily, ready for pie.

I remember our fingers making crow feet on the edges of the pie crust. Mixed in with the apple slices: pears, cinnamon sticks, a four-leaf clover plucked from a plant by the sink. Four knife holes to allow for air to enter, so the sweet goo bubbles only partially to the surface. Next come guests.

Your doorbell won't stop ringing, the counters filled with dishes and cling-wrapped cookie plates, everything frosted and blue for the season, all the meat carved into thin disks, the wine uncorked, bundles of silverware tied together with thick, red ribbons; no one color coordinates better than lonely academics around the holidays. There are tinsel bundles connected to gold wires and taped above every doorway; pastel paper stars, music, and warm boots. Puddles of melted snow by the doorway, the house lit golden from within, you can barely hear it, the wind, but it's there, pressing snowflakes against the glass screens and porch door. No one needs to worry about your cat escaping, because she's hiding under the table, eating turkey coated in jam.

For a long time, it's all love. Someone brings up the deer boy; everyone laughs about magic and mayhem.

"We can't keep meeting like this," says Frank, a professor of sociology. He's tall and curly haired with tortoiseshell glasses and one dimple in his left cheek.

"You mean drunk on Christmas Eve?" you ask, already pouring him more scotch.

"Exactly. Why don't we hang out more during the school year?"

You pretend not to notice he's flirting with you; we exchange a look and you shrug. Your sweater is the exact hue and softness of an overripe tomato. I consider eating you in one bite, maybe two, if there's time.

"We should probably drink a little less if we don't want to be talked about at the next faculty meeting," says my mother, but what does she know? She's only ever taught theater to high schoolers; she's never had to endure what we have endured.

Someone brings a basket of overripe berries, and I think I recognize baneberries, doll's-eyes, and bittersweet belladonnas, but the bearer places the basket in the center of the table, instructs us not to touch its contents. I want to, so badly, can feel my tongue bending over backwards to escape my teeth. You are nowhere to be found, left my mother alone to entertain academics. Jules is uncorking wine, asks me to help you bring the rest of the glasses from the attic. I can't help thinking it's a trick. She's going to poison us when we're back, the scent masked behind a particularly fruity Malbec. I can hear her now, hyperfocused on the nose: vanilla scones and Saturday afternoons, cinnamon-hued holiday cookies, maybe snickerdoodle bitten through with hothouse tomatoes, birch, all those earthly scents eaten by the grapes, plucked by the farmers.

I wish I had a cigarette. I wish I understood gentleness. Could I love you the way you need me to, could I explain myself for once? Recognize my face in the faux-gold mirror out front, the one you require all guests to look into so as to allow the spirits to keep track of who (or what) enters your space—who is coming and going?

When I reach the second-floor landing, I find not you but a series of clocks all pointing to twelve, a black-and-white photograph of the most selfish person we know in all of New York City (nicknamed Santi, real name: Saint.) I remember this day vividly. Your suppressed emotions, Santi shaving his head in the old kitchen sink with hot and cold water always coming out opposite. He'd blown out all the candles you lit, claimed they quickened his pulse ("but not in the good way"). Where are you, I wonder, not just in the house but in your art? Does there not come a time of reflection, even in all that observation?

You are on the third floor, back to the staircase, collarbone protruding like wings, all the little pebbles in your spine making the pattern of an oceanic anchor, your skin light brown and freckled but only on your arms. When I reach you, after what feels like ages, I find you're snacking on a mushy peach and flipping through a half-abandoned sketch pad. Wineglasses lie abandoned in their crepe paper coffins. A hazy look swirls in your eyes.

"Jess?" I say (though it's more accurate to relay the word *whisper*, because sometimes saying your name feels like a spell to wake the dead).

"Mm," you respond, not diverting your gaze from the book. "Do you remember any of these?"

I have this terrible habit of holding my breath whenever you're around, realizing it later, only after I've become lightheaded, heart trilling like mourning doves.

There are drawings of lake ice and sea ice, also known as black ice, and frail, greasy, blue needles; blue herons with outstretched wings, an egret eating, pelicans we once saw snickering into their cove.

"Jules was asking about the wineglasses," I say, as if that's a sufficient apology for my half-melted gestures, shaking hands. Each page I lift trembles.

I wonder if your ex ever taught you spells to coax art to life. I should have warned you Jules sent me, though I'm sure you know, always so focused on your friends' habits. Jules prefers to obsess over strangers; I comb through new hiding spaces, obsessing over where to hide my awful body. At every social event in your house: the linen closet, pantry, under your bed, not the shed with cat-fur-soft spiders, yes in the cabinet with the garbage disposal switch, sometimes behind your newly stretched canvases.

"What happened to us?"

I'm so startled by your question, I don't pause to think you could be referring to our mutual abandonment of art, you after an accident with your hands, me after I found writing was a better outlet to speak to you.

"Art is nauseating," I say, and you nod, as if this is what we have been trying to get to all along, the revelation that abandonment is good, especially when we're doing the abandoning, when we are in control.

But I'm not in control, and the only reason I don't reach for your face is the footsteps in the hall, small creaking noises, the shuffle of a body thumping against the wall. I think of my own dizzy and distracted walk and wonder who might be lurking outside the door. You get up first, perhaps ticked off at the disruption; instead there is nothing. Yes, the barest howl of wind; yes, the amber hallway of newly stained wood; yes, holes for mice. Yes to the ghost, just say yes, admit you know this house is haunted, by what? The answer remains unclear. The love that died between us, the ghost of my mother's history, escaped through her mouth during a fit of laughter; maybe there are ghosts in the pie, and poisons in the berry patches. By the time dinner ends, we'll all be poltergeists, excitedly fleeing to haunt our respective families, sisters of sisters, brothers who don't care, and fathers who taught the mothers they don't matter.

I have an intrusive thought you will turn around and half your face will be missing, or your teeth will be replaced with fangs. You will eat me where I kneel. I pick up a discarded paintbrush with a sharpened edge, make a mental note to ask you about this later, hold it tightly in my hand, remind myself I can kill you if I need to, if you're possessed, if you're demon, if you're out of mercy.

You turn and your face is love. I ask if you're possessed, and you laugh, tell me you need to start keeping track of the hauntings; perhaps you'll return to art. You ask me why the pencil is in my hand.

I show you it's a paintbrush, and your face grows hard and wooden in that way I know you love, when you're trying to protect your mind and me at the same time.

"Oh," you say, taking the brush out of my hand.

To my surprise, you toss it in the trash.

"Let's return to dinner," you tell me.

* * *

This is the part where dinner fades blue-green red. The part where I try to figure out if you were possessed, this time by some type of love spirit. I try to figure out if my wife was the one on the staircase, somehow swift enough to hide before you turned the knob. When did the door close? Has the attic always had a door? There are pictures of your mother and father in the dining room, but someone has scratched off your father's face like a lottery ticket. I, too, cannot remember my own father's face; if forced or pressed, I would draw a scribble, a chaos, or perhaps an oblong, an absence, void, trick, wish, puff of smoke. Used to taste his coffee when mother wasn't looking, taking gentle sips of vanilla cream, dipped my crackers in the hot liquid and sucked on them until I developed cavities. Still, what did his face look like? Has he been following me around all this time, or am I in that space again, mixing up monsters with family, mistaking a boogeyman beneath my bed for a friend?

You told me not to get twisted up in my past, and I recall I got pissed off. It's something I can't help, nor can I justify it, like all the leftover love I feel for you—we've got to come up with a better word; four letters isn't enough to encompass the feeling of my face being shoved underwater each time you look my way. Wear sunglasses, would you? The blue is practically stolen from the sea.

My wife pours wine. I'm having those thoughts again, of poison and magic. After dinner my body will transform into a green parrot and fly away to Broadway, where I'll hang out on gum-stained streets, sleep on sun-soaked stoops, eat leftover soft pretzels in Central Park. I drink the wine as quickly as possible, but my arms remain where they are, no feathers, no green like emeralds, my eyes still dark brown but not black, not small and round like little coals. Oh well, I think.

There are tea cakes the color of ash. Rivulets of apples, pineapple muffins, a dish coated in almonds and half-submerged apple slices, a cloth basket carrying a vanilla loaf filled with walnuts. Someone is scooping pistachio ice cream, there is custard, there is this strange desire to eat extra-rare meat, I am craving bacon, I want to tear apart the dinner table with my fingers and teeth. I get crumbs on my chin, everything is softened butter and frozen raspberries in small ceramic bowls, I want to be ground to a fine paste or a pile of dust, you are looking at me like you're the pestle, eager to make me into syrup.

My wife, lovely and distracted, isn't eating. She lets her fingers brush the top of the cakes, scrunches her nose at strawberry frosting in place of cinnamon. She looks lonely, and I want to excuse myself to sit next to her. I feel a strange grape seed of love forming in my chest, blossoming into a branch, but I'm selfish. I impale too many people with my affections, my arms are hard and bony, this is my fault, my body feels yellow in a way I can't explain.

turns, sees me, and immediately dashes across the building towards the plaza. In chase, I see him drop off the horizon. He simply ran out of roof. Unfortunately, I realized this midair, while I too didn't stop in time.

Off the edge and airborne, I fall hard into a dumpster next to an unconscious would-be thief. Thank heavens we hit a dumpster filled with insulation leftover from a store in progress of a remodel. We had a relatively soft landing. Soaked from watery plaster, pieces of glass, and pink insulation, an assortment of crap sticks to almost every inch of my body, head to toe. I'm a human collage. Despite our appearance, I cuff my rooftop marauder and port him to the station for booking. I'm happy to get one thief off the street. No doubt there are more lurking a round this small town.

I head home after my shift. Tessie hears my car enter the driveway. She opens the front door and begins shaking her head. "You can't come into the house like that! I know there's a dark navy blue uniform under that slime somewhere!"

Under her breath I can hear her talking to herself: "*Ya tenemos una hija. Eres como otro bebé del que tengo que limpiar,*" meaning "We already have a daughter. You're like another baby I have to clean up after."

In practical Northern Arizona fashion, she grabs the hose and starts to spray me down. I have to laugh the whole damn time as my lovely, caring wife makes me suitable for entering the house.

A couple years go by and we are in the same situation, facing store break ins in our commercial district. Officers are assigned in the same way as done previously. One of my shifts is reminiscent of my first encounter on the rooftops. This time while I'm stationed on a rooftop, a youth jumps over the false front of the building's façade and lands directly in front of me. Face to face, he's temporarily paralyzed, then makes a mad dash along the rooftops heading toward the plaza.

He jumps across a small alley, rolling onto the roof of the next building. I clear the gap as well. As I roll to a stop, he's getting up and resumes his sprint.

We quickly approach the end of the roof. There's a fire escape ladder on the other side of the street. The guy jumps for it, but fails to catch a rung and lands hard on the street below. I can make it, I say to myself, and take a leap of faith. I actually catch a rung with one hand, but I'm not strong enough to hold on long. I grasp for another rung, but only my finger tips touch the metal bar. I hit the pavement so hard I think the cement cracked.

Now there's two of us lying groggy on the ground. I muster the strength to cuff the young man and ask a store owner to call an ambulance and for another squad car to come to the scene. A few minutes later, Officer Rivera pulls up and takes custody of our injured guest. I tell Rivera that I don't need to go to the hospital . . . not the smartest decision I have ever made.

At the end of the shift, I head home. I can hardly

move and enter the front door somewhat in the gait of Quasimodo—the hunchback of Notre Dame. Tessie comes to my side, assisting me into our living room lounge chair. She asks for details about what happened to me, mainly about my physical condition. I convince her that by tomorrow I'll be fine.

Tessie gets me two aspirins and water, then helps me get into the shower. While waiting for the water temperature to warm, she reminds me that we have plans to run errands in town in the early morning.

When I get up to face the day, I can hardly move, aching all over. Slowly moving arms into sleeves and legs into pants, it takes me twenty minutes just to get dressed. I start walking toward the car like a *viejito*—a little old man. Tessie opens the passenger side door for me. As soon as she gets into the driver's seat, she turns toward me and begins a conversation.

She asks, "Are you an expert in narcotics?"

"No," I answer, "I'm not very good in that area."

"Are you the fastest runner on the force?"

I say "No, I am not the fastest runner. Far from it."

Her logic becomes obvious when she looks straight into my eyes and comments: "You realize this is the second time you fall off a rooftop. Since you are not good at rooftop jogging, I suggest that you don't ever do it again."

Over the years, I've learned that scolding is one of the many ways my dear Tessie expresses her love for me.

Mommy is Sleeping

Late January. It's snowing lightly. We are working the graveyard shift so we had come to the office about 8:00pm and we work until 6:00am, working "four tens," which is when we work four ten-hour shifts, combining days off and on Friday, Saturday and Sunday. We rotate our schedule so we work weekends for three months and then have the following three months off on weekends.

This evening just after our scheduled briefing, we get a call about three very young children who called to order pizza from Geppetto's downtown location. The owner relayed what a child told him on the phone.

"They are very hungry. Their mother is sleeping. They call her name and shake her, but she doesn't wake up. The children don't know their address and weren't quite sure where they live."

A few in the department know the downtown area very well and figure the children and mother must frequent the pizzeria fairly often. They probably don't live too far away. What homes in the immediate area have children? A couple officers move out to investigate a few possible locations.

Two officers go to an apartment on the south side where they know three children live with their mom, a single parent. The apartment is not in the better part of town. They knock on the door and a five-year-old lets them enter. A terrible, rank oder assaults their sense of smell. They know immediately that the mother has been dead for some days.

The officers start to closely inspect each room. The children had managed to eat everything that they could find: bread, cereal, celery, carrots, etc. The youngest child must be only two years old. The children tried their best to provide for themselves while trying to wake their mom. Of course, the mother wouldn't wake up, so they eventually even tried to open canned goods. They tried and tried to open them, using knives, forks, and other utensils.

This is when the officers find out who's on call to access the scene. They need a coroner and also a state certified social worker to come to the apartment and tell us where to take the children—a professional who cares for foster kids in emergency situations.

One social worker was contacted by phone. She tells the sergeant: "Look, I'd like to come, but it's too dangerous. I can't drive in this kind of weather. It's snowing hard now and the roads are frozen over with black ice."

She's right. Snow nears the top of our boots, about halfway between our ankle and mid-calf. The social worker makes a suggestion. "You guys are there. Can't you just pick somebody to bring the children to the station?"

At this time of night, there's not many people to turn to for help. The officers narrow down the options to the captain—that's me. At midnight, there's no other person on the totem pole available. I'm not highest on the list, but at midnight, a captain is at the top of the list of people that are in charge of the city. We can't contact the higher-ups, the mayor, assistant mayor, or other department heads. So I get on over to the apartment and we act quickly.

First is to get some food for the children and officers. We call Geppetto's and catch the man who had just cleaned and is ready to close up. When he hears of our situation, he heats up the oven again and makes a couple of pizzas for the kids and the officers. He delivers two large pizzas for free. We need milk for the children, especially the two youngest babies. I have a daughter who is five, the same age as the eldest child. I understand the childrens' needs.

Now, I turn my attention to the mother, laying motionless on the livingroom couch with a needle hanging out of her arm. She is easy to evaluate and is cold dead. We don't see any outward signs of foul play. The medical examiner, more commonly known as a corner, and two nurses, are on their way. They are having trouble trying to get through the snow themselves. They are volunteers that are trained just for this purpose. They come out to the scene and pronounce the person dead, then give instructions as to who to call to remove the body, usually a funeral home.

I am waiting for the medical examiner to cover her up. The needle is still in the discolored arm.

In the meantime, I discuss with the sergeant who first arrived on the scene just what we should do now with the children. No social supervisor is available because of the storm. It's Thursday and we need to figure out where the children can stay over the weekend.

By now it's about 1:30 in the morning. Who can I call for advice? Of course, the only one who comes to mind is my wife, Tessie. The phone's ring wakes her up. She's worried about me, but I assure her, " I'm fine, but I have a problem: I have three little girls in need." She gives a quick response, saying "Get them to me."

"How am I gonna get the children to you? The roads everywhere are a foot deep in snow."

Sweet Tessie demands, "Braden Joseph, you're the chief! Get some snow plows out and clear the roads!"

At first I think she's out of her mind. After a few phone calls, I'm surprised at the rapid response. Those in charge of the various city, state, and county roads, all jump in to help. They all sympathize with the childrens' predicament, their mother dying, and in need of a place to stay. The plowmen organize. With three little tikes sitting cozily in my back seat, I follow plows from the apartment directly to my front door. Tessie is waiting. Hot milk and cookies are at the table.

My wife made some calls on Friday explaining our position to state officials. The children will stay with us through Monday then, of course, we will to turn them over to Protective Services.

Power of Love

Another late night routine. I'm out on the road patrolling the streets. My car is quietly idling in a store parking lot off the road. I'm between two traffic lights, one at San Isidro and the other at College Park Avenue.

It's one of those summer nights when the air has cooled some and feels great with a window open. With the car window down, I hear a car coming quickly in my direction. It is traveling at high velocity, twice the posted speed limit. I look up to witness a green Ford fly right through both traffic lights.

At 4:00 in the morning, there is no traffic. I turn on the siren and close in on my target. The driver, a female, pulls over and I ask for her drivers license, insurance, and registration. I'm doing my duty, focused on meting out justice and writing out the appropriate tickets.

I move closer to the vehicle to hand the young lady her citations and notice she's crying. Perhaps she's upset for the penalties she'll have to pay.

Going by the book, I say, "Miss, if you have any questions about the citations, you have one week to contact our office."

She thanks me and speaks in a whimper, "I just got a call that my son is not doing well. He's at St. Mary's Hospital. I was trying to get there as quick as I could."

There was something about the way she looked at me in tears and I knew she wasn't lying.

I head back to the station. It's about 6 o'clock

when I start turning in my paperwork. I tell the sergeant what happened. He immediately asks, "Did you check with the hospital on the boy's condition?"

When I shake my head indicating I hadn't, he hands me the phone on his desk. "Call them."

Staff at Saint Mary's respond quickly, verifying "The mother did arrive, apologizing for being delayed."

I don't bother to explain to the hospital staff that it is I who am responsible for her not arriving sooner. Hit with guilt, I feel so bad my stomach becomes upset.

Instead of going home when my shift ends at 7:00am, I decided to go speak with the city judge. I wait an hour for him to arrive at his office.

When he arrives, I tell him about the young lady, the speeding tickets, and the citations for running two red lights. In addition, I relate the story of the son being at the hospital. However, my main reason for being there is to ask him if it is possible to cancel the citations.

"Well officer," he asks, "did you go to the hospital to verify her story?"

"No Sir, but I did call Saint Mary's and they did say she was there and the son was in an operating room."

The judge stares at his desk a few lengthy seconds. He looks up and says he'll take care of the tickets, then asks me, "Did you learn anything from this incident?"

"Well, from now on, I'm gonna ask anyone who runs a traffic light why they did so. I'll ask them to tell me what happened. Then I'll evaluate whether they're telling me the truth or not. In some ways, tonight's work has made a big difference on how I will relate to the public from now on."

The judge's face shows approval. "Good to hear Officer Vicentin. Contact the young lady and let her know that the charges have been dropped. And, these pink papers, signed by me, are for your records stating that this case is closed."

The Distinguishing Mark

Now I lay me down to sleep... So many nights like this, alone with my thoughts of the day. As a policeman's wife, each night is the same, praying my husband stays safe on the job. I've learned of the all too many dangers he faces daily, the sacrifices he makes, and the toll it takes on him physically and mentally. I've never needed an alarm clock to wake up in the mornings. The sound of Braden's car returning home is enough.

When he does make it home from work, my first question is always "How was the shift?" This question is usually made internally in an emotional silence. Over the years, I've listened to hundreds of his abbreviated reports, many very mundane and others just harrowing. But I know there are hundreds of stories I have not heard. Some stories he would never share. It takes a special psyche to bear the most terrifying experiences. Also, I'm sure a number of stories remain untold because of his humility. He selflessly has helped so many people without acknowledgment by others.

As every police officer, Braden has his tales of law enforcement. They are insightful. A Native American leader and warrior in the Midwest, Black Hawk, once wrote: "Take only memories, leave only footprints." The tales record a vital part of our lives and community. The experience can be transmitted so others can benefit.

I look forward to when Braden retires from the police force. He'll no doubt continue to work, semi-retired, perhaps in a relatively safer position that can utilize his talents. But, we will have more time together, sharing family time with our lovely teenage daughter Almarosa. We can finally make time for fun activities, attend cultural events, and even take exotic vacations on a tropical island!

Every day I'm thankful for my husband as a human being, a family man, and someone dedicated to his job. Decades ago I fell in love with him because of his character, a rich mix of compassion, empathy, intelligence, and energy. It earned him respect at work and in the community, along with deep love at home. He has the rare ability to adapt, as he did since moving here from the East Coast, fully embracing our heritage. He has blended the East and West, the past and the present. He's spiced up our lives, much like green and red chili!

I'm always amazed at how Braden has been able to perform as a policeman and to be such a wonderful family man. It really isn't a profound mystery how he's done it. His heart is his badge.

POLICE

Notes

Did you enjoy reading

Crossfire Southwest!

As a collection of short fictional stories, this book has a focus on law enforcement with accounts of cops, robbers, drunks, and bikers. There are also accounts of compassion for the public, comradery among fellow officers, and love of family. I am always fascinated by the interaction of peoples from different cultural backgrounds as in the Southwest. If you have benefited by reading this book, your honest feedback on Amazon would be appreciated.

To write a short review:
    1) use your camera app
    2) take a photo of the QR code below
    3) a review page will open in your web browser
OR
    Visit **Amazon.com**, search *Crossfire Southwest*, and click on "Review this product."

Thank you much!

What you don't know about the leaving is I'm a goldfinch sailing through the window. Behind me I can hear laughter and screaming, this is a party trick, I'll be back in time to roast the potatoes in garlic and chives, I'll draw up my silk pajamas at dinnertime and fashion a beautiful blue bow out of the cords, we'll see each other again, we'll buy butter knives in winter in Boston, ornaments from that place you love so much below Grand Central Station, where the ornaments hang in the window like frosted pastries coated in thick layers of glitter and confetti, each more delicate than the last, everything is so expensive but it won't matter, because I'll be human and alive. Which isn't to say I'm not animal and alive on this classic fall day. The air smells like my past, and I can almost see my ex-girlfriends filtering through the door in their burnt-orange sweaters, everyone has a different flavor of pumpkin pie, don't they know I hate that dessert, everyone has glossy apple earrings, they make jokes with my wife, they make jokes with you, everyone is saying it's not a sin to love more than one person, I should be free.

* * *

Freed. With beak and black stripe, I go searching for berries. Did you know there are dreams of birds? In the dreams of birds there are worms. There are different words for sunshine and sunlight, incapable of being translated into human speech. Everything is the color of honey pears, we can smell apple trees from miles away, we steal shortbread from windowsills and miss vanilla bean lattes but love raw vanilla beans, cracking between our beaks like Pop Rocks. In the dreams of birds are our exes, for every bird was once a human, but not every human has been poisoned to be a bird, it seems that's only my fate, I can't figure out where the spell was hidden. Tucked away into cream? Taking the form of the walnut I overchewed between my back molars, perhaps it was in the demi-sec, the moelleux, my obsession Chenin Blanc, all ribs and so sweet it turned my rib cage light pink. That morning she cooked me hash browns with over-easy eggs, I had avocado toast with spices, I ate omelets, perhaps it was my last meal, the food before the seeds, no more huevos rancheros, for I am a bird and I eat from the earth, but I still remember the way you liked to eat your porridge, burnt slightly on the top until a golden skin had formed, you'd joke and pretend to crack the edge like crème brûlée, I knew I loved you then, at the breakfast table, but when I was about to tell you, my wife walked into the room and asked how we were enjoying our morning meals, could she get us more coffee, sweet smile, her eyes rimmed with recent weeping, a sour phone call with her mother, or perhaps she'd known, before either of us had, that things would always end this way, a rush and ride of the wind, too-green forest, farewell over my shoulder, brief glance of my wife, pissed off she poisoned the wrong woman, tipping over dessert trays, sending forks and knives flying into the pressed shirts and knit sweaters of unsuspecting academics.

Sam Moe has received residencies from VCCA and Château d'Orquevaux. She is the recipient of a 2023 St. Joe Community Foundation Poetry Fellowship from Longleaf Writers Conference. Her work has appeared or is forthcoming in *Peatsmoke Journal*, *The Indianapolis Review*, *Sundog Lit*, and others. Her first full-length collection, *Heart Weeds*, was published with Alien Buddha Press (Sept. '22) and her second full-length collection, *Grief Birds*, was published with Bullshit Lit (Apr. '23). Her third full-length collection, *Cicatrizing the Daughters*, is forthcoming from FlowerSong Press.

Shellfish

Me,
tattooed
on your skin.
You weren't after new ink,
you've already turned your ex's initial
into a bird in flight, feathers scattered
down your arm. Sketch me, a hermit crab
lodging in a home never my own. Me, concealed
in a spiral of pigmented calcium carbonate
for our protection.
For my protection.
A spiral of pigmented calcium carbonate
conceals: home is never my own. I'm lodged in
a hermit crab sketch on your arm.
Scattered feathers. A bird took flight,
returned to your ex's initial
ink. You weren't after
new skin.

Seabird

The gulf on a dodge tide.
Is this the sanctuary you seek?
A shore of sharp edges:
seashell, crab, splintered bone.
A sheol of invertebrates.
A feast of squirm and scuttle—
transparent husk, red veins, dark guts.
A sea too shallow for the monster cuttlefish you dreamed.

Flock and dapple the waters edge, dredge—
Bathe your wounds, iodine
black in the kelp and krill:
Is there no solace without salt?
A glut of lice and driftwood
and you lie, quivering on the mud?
Are there not enough feathers here scattered,
shafts plucked clean by the turbulence of sand?

Make your nest inland. Find any twisted mallee,
any stand of knotted roadside grass.
Build sandhills in the guttergrime and content yourself
with that.
You have no need of shoaling.

You have no need of another's breast-bone pressed into
your wing.
You have no need of another's beak, pressing fermented
mullet into your own squalling maw.

No.

Sit with the hollow of your bones.
Sit with your tattered wings, your transparent squirm.
Watch the tide ebb, and ebb and flow.

I didn't intend to become the ocean—

just a raindrop to nestle in her hair. Yet gravity and the moon conspired and drew me deeper: creek stream, river shattered over the cliffs, lake—and now—I am murky depths, confused currents and filthy foam spit, laden with salt rising to whip and burn. Fury and greed, I lust after the earth, I would take her in my arms, my mouth, I would swallow her, I would endlessly caress her edges— Oh my love. I can keep your nightmares safe, welcome your monsters into my belly, my caves, resplendent with ancient treasure and soft-edged glass the color of the forests. Let me nurture your small transparent jelly-offspring with algae-crumbs pulled from the path of moonlight, nurture them til they grow chitin armor or cuttle-bone and tentacles, til they are ready for the ravages of rock and air. When they are ready I will kiss them each and remind them: i am eternal for your returning.

At the sunrise I will open myself to yellow and gold, I will open my ears to the cry of the silver gull, the osprey, the keening allocasuarina. They will tell me, sing to me of you and I will drink my fill of liquid song and cry soft mist to find you. When it is quiet in the evening, allow yourself to hear my breath: rhythmic i rise and fall away—in the

depth of the silence between, know what my absence
would be: for there is a desert where I am but crushed shell
and baked salt, pink with iron-stained tears.

Ubajee Lookout

There are no wolves here so my son makes them up, makes us up into a pack, Nominates an alpha. *I want to be the cub!—but then I won't be able to lead.* If I follow him, we will likely migrate. Follow some rabbit trail that takes us to the moon.

The moon! he echoes, yellow eyes already tracing trajectories, an instinctive trigonometry of astrological contour lines. If we were on the moon, what would inspire our howl?

Don't howl now, the sun is still up, wolves live like shadows amongst the trees. We hide behind the grass tree while hikers pass. They are geared up, matching khaki, compasses and maps in clear weatherproof pockets. My son and I in just our sleek summer coats with an idea that at the bottom of the gully there should be a stream, the stream should run to the ocean, and the ocean will birth the sun, and we will call that place East.

When we find the creek, will there be snacks? I tell him we will hunt fish in the stream, catch them in our mouths as they leap. Rainbow sashimi. There are no salmon in this stream, only glistening dreams to be caught in our bare teeth, and savored.

A Date At The Market

with a sushi chef from Moonta Bay: locks, nose-ring and seal-round eyes. She bought herself a decaf latte and you a cappuccino. Instead of raising the cup to your lip you plunge your spoon, twist, scoop froth, submerge again. She talks of single origin but all you can think about is foam, the way it mounds and crescents and how would it be, to be with her? All rising and ebbing tides, quiet in the shelter between peninsulae? Or surf coast, an open ocean hunt? What sort of creature do you find yourself to be—have you grown fat and fur? If you are in your scales beware—this ends with your salmon flesh translucent against her knife.

Kathryn Reese lives in South Australia. She works in medical science. Her writing explores themes of nature, myth and the possibility of shape shift. Her poems are published in Neoperennial Press's "Heroines" Anthology, *Paperbark, Hayden's Ferry Review,* and *Yellow Arrow Journal.* You can find her on Instagram @katwhetter and on Twitter @KathrynRwReese

Interview with Mary Otis

By A.M. Larks

Mary Otis took time out during her holiday travels to catch up with me via email. Her debut novel Burst is a buzz and after attending a reading on her book tour, I wanted to know more. I wanted to know how. I wanted to know why. And true to form, my former professor did not disappoint.

[Kelp Journal] The structure of *Burst*—with the nonchronological arrangement of chapters—is so interesting, and as you know, I am partial to a fragmented narrative. But I was particularly taken with the fact that in *Burst* certain chapters act as flashbacks, while the main narrative is moving forward in time. I know it may be simple and is likely well-known, but the fact that a chapter could be a flashback blew my mind. It made me wonder, How did this novel come into being? Specifically, was this arrangement of fragmented time part of how you drafted your novel in the first place, or was this structure determined later in editing?

[**Mary Otis**] In many ways nonlinear storytelling can illuminate the truth of lived experience more powerfully than one that moves forward chronologically. For example, and this speaks to interior life, a person or character might be waiting in line at the post office, but mentally they're submerged in a day twenty years ago. If you were to unscrew anyone's head, you might be surprised by where their mind resides because so often it is not the present. Additionally, while *Burst* is a novel, I've written many short stories and am naturally pulled to begin a narrative in the middle of things rather than at the chronological beginning.

I often talk to my ninety-nine-year-old neighbor, who has led a remarkable, beautiful life, but one that is not without tragedy. She frequently recalls significant memories, and they're never chronological in terms of actual dates, but there is always a throughline in terms of the emotional connections. I think this is also the case with characters relative to memory.

A lot of the initial material in *Burst* came to me out of order, and then once I connected those passages, I built the structure to support it. While there are a few flashback chapters in the novel, my aim with each one was to provide further crucial information only when necessary and when there was a natural springboard or subtextual link. This was particularly helpful in terms of illuminating a character like Charlotte, who is troubled and troubling. When a reader gets a glimpse of her earlier life, it helps put some of her behavior in context. Lastly, by using a nonlinear structure, I was able to cut back and forth in time and cover a sweep of three decades more easily than if it had been linear.

[KJ] Another interesting part of your book is the addition of an author's note, which is basically a reference page of the nonfiction resources you used as sources of not only information but inspiration. I loved Joan Acocella's *Twenty-Eight Artists and Two Saints* as well, and you mention that Vivian Maier's *Untitled, 1956* was a particular source of inspiration. How did these other art forms aid and inspire *Burst*?

[MO] There is a Lorrie Moore quote about writing a story that I love: "First comes some idea, then things fall in from the world, things that have correspondence to the first idea and eventually there's a moment when the story closes or shuts and becomes a hothouse of a fictional world." I find this to be very true whether the things that "fall in" are from real life or from the inspiration and timing of a piece of art one encounters while writing. So much of a writer's job seems to be about intention and availability, and when I'm working on something, the world can begin to take on a porous aspect in a very beneficial way.

During the writing of *Burst*, I discovered Maier's photography, and *Untitled, 1956* had a profound effect on me and served as an artistic talisman during the writing of my novel. The subject, a woman in a red dress, stands with her back to the camera, hands clasped in a way that on different days seemed to signal different things— anticipation, longing, atonement. The photo prompted me to write an entire chapter of my novel. I'm grateful for this kind of mysterious convergence when it occurs, this cross inspiration of art forms.

[**KJ**] I was taken with the seamless narration of Viva in *Burst* as she ages from a child just on the verge of middle school to a full-blown adult. That seems to be a particularly hard task. What did you consider in order to achieve that I-am-old-but-still-me voice? Was that any different than your approach to the variety of narrators you employed for *Yes, Yes, Cherries?*

[**MO**] I did theater when I was younger, and I often approach creating a character in the same way as if I was playing that character (in terms of background, desires, hang-ups, secrets, and what is most at stake). Not all of this will be apparent on the page, but it will inform the actions my characters take, what they reveal, what they hide. Whenever I'm writing a character, I'm always on their side in terms of what they want even, and especially if, there are numerous characters with whom they are in conflict, as is the case in this novel. I don't think you can write what you don't understand, so I always need to have some kind of inner appreciation or empathy for a character in order to write that character. If I can sustain that throughout a short story or novel, then it's possible to illuminate the entirety of the character's life on the page.

[**KJ**] One of the things that struck me about both *Burst* and *Yes, Yes, Cherries* was the complexity of the relationships you describe. Everything is constantly in flux, pushing and pulling, ebbing and flowing, like the tides. Everything also builds on what has come before, exponentially. Do you think all of our relationships (friendships, lovers, family) are subject to these same mathematical and scientific forces?

[MO] I do. When I write, cause and effect are always in the back of my mind. What does a particular action or line of dialogue engender, and how does that link to the next emotional pivot point? It's also one of the most organic ways to approach plot and structure rather than trying to jam a preconceived idea or template on top of the writing.

When you're young, it's hard to comprehend the extent to which things can change and how truly elastic and unpredictable human nature can be. I enjoy exploring that, and fluidity is central to the novel not only in terms of shifting alliances but quite literally in terms of dance. I think it would be rare to find a relationship that is completely fixed and unchanging, although it might be an interesting exercise to try and write about one!

[KJ] *Burst* tackles the issue of substance abuse head-on without being derivative or cliché. When conceiving these characters, did you always have in mind something like this to connect them? Something both genetic and environmental? Something attributable to both nurture and nature?

[MO] One of the things I explore in the novel is genetic predisposition as it intersects with artistic purpose. I always knew that Charlotte grappled with addiction, but I initially didn't plan that her daughter would as well. But as the plot developed, it seemed like it had to happen, particularly as the character has in some ways defined herself against her mother. Ultimately, she must face the question of whether she's able to change her own genetic wiring. While Viva is an artist, a dancer, one might say that her mother, Charlotte, is an artist without an art form. I was interested in looking at what happens when an artistic impulse is thwarted and how that can play out in dangerous ways. When the novel opens, we're in a car with Viva and Charlotte barreling down the "suicide lane," a lane in which cars can pass going in both directions. That opening image speaks to the risk and inherent danger of addiction and the necessary risks that need to be taken to flourish as an artist.

[**KJ**] Humor is always apparent in all of your writing, and *Burst* is no exception. In my own experience, it can be easier to wield in a shorter work than a longer one. Is this your experience as well?

[**MO**] That's an interesting question, because humor often hinges on specificity, precision, and brevity, and those aspects are integral to any short story. However, I didn't experience a significant shift relative to humor as it works in a longer form. A friend of mine has synesthesia— a phenomenon where one sees letters in colors—and this is something like how I see the world relative to humor. I find it fairly difficult not to see the humor in something, even in the most trying of circumstances.

[KJ] I was particular struck by one part of *Burst*: Viva is in her classroom, meditating on teaching, and the passage begins, "Viva worked hard to locate something within each girl—a fierceness, or sorrow, or anger, and wake her up to the fact that she could use that energy as a vehicle." The paragraph ends with this singular question: "What good was an inner life if no one could see it?" It felt like a call to arms. I think about this line every time I sit down to write, for what else are writers doing but sharing their innermost selves? I have to know: Whatever inspired this haunting insight?

[MO] Interestingly, the dancers in that scene are more invested in the surface of things, the presentation of the art form and its outward appearances rather than what they might specifically bring to it. So, I meant that line— in this particular context and in view of our very outward-facing culture—ironically. However, I love your interpretation, and it's a good reminder that all art is interactive. There is an artist who creates something, and then there is the reader or viewer who receives it and brings their own impressions to the table. The goal of transmuting inner life through words or paint or movement is a very worthy one, and certainly, it's a rather alchemical process.

[**KJ**] *Burst* is such an interesting title. Things burst at the seams, others burst forth, and of course, bubbles burst. Where did this wonderful, enticing one-word title come from?

[**MO**] The title came to me in the middle of the night, and while it appeared like a blinking light in my subconscious, I didn't initially know how it applied to the novel. Those things took some time to discover. Readers have pointed out to me that characters are bursting, busting, imploding. The first use of the word *burst* in the novel refers to Viva dancing and feeling like she's left the confines of her body. When Charlotte departs this Earth, there is a line that she "bursts free of the human cage." There is also a theme that runs through the book relative to the exploration of the things from which numerous characters must break free.

Prior to the title *Burst*, I employed two other "ghost" titles, both of which served me well in writing aspects of the novel. Each of those titles seemed to "wear out" once I'd written certain passages, but they were very helpful in pulling me forward. I love thinking about titles, and there is something about seeing any title day after day that works in a mysterious, energetic way. It's like when you're in grade school and write the name of a crush again and again on a piece of paper. The words seen to grow in power and depth.

Lastly, while a bubble might burst, as it does for Viva, bubbles can also be confining, and I think that in her case, as painful as it might be, once this occurs, her landscape of possibility expands exponentially, and hope becomes manifest.

Mary Otis is the author of the novel, *Burst* (Zibby Books), which is longlisted for the 2024 Joyce Carol Oates Prize and won the 2023 Silver Medal in Literary Fiction from the Independent Book Publisher Awards. Burst was chosen by Good Morning America, the *New York Post* and *The Orange County Register* as one of the Best Books of Spring 2023. Mary has also published a short story collection, *Yes, Yes, Cherries* (Tin House). Her stories and essays have been published in *Best New American Voices, Tin House, Electric Literature, McSweeney's, Los Angeles Times, Los Angeles Review of Books*, and in many literary journals and numerous anthologies. She has recently published poetry in *Zyzzyva* and the *Bennington Review. The New York Times* has said of her work, "Sadness and humor sidle up to each other, evocative of the delicate balance of melancholy and wit found in Lorrie Moore's stories." Her story "Pilgrim Girl" received an Honorable Mention for the Pushcart Prize, and her story "Unstruck" was a Distinguished Story of the Year in *Best American Short Stories.* She was a Walter Dakin Fellow and received a Getty Foundation Scholarship. Mary has read her work at Lincoln Center and was filmed for the PBS Program "Brief but Spectacular." She attended Bennington College and previously taught creative writing in the UCLA Writers' Program in addition to numerous writing conferences. Mary was a founding fiction professor in the UC Riverside Low-Residency MFA Program where she taught for twelve years. Originally from the Boston area, Mary lives in Los Angeles. www.maryotis.com

---

A.M. Larks's writing has appeared in *NiftyLit, Scoundrel Time, Assay: A Journal of Nonfiction Studies, Five on the Fifth, Charge Magazine,* and he *ZYZZYVA* and *Ploughshares* blogs. She has served as a judge for the Loud Karma Productions' Emerging Female and Nonbinary Playwriting Award and has performed her stories at Lit Up at Town Hall Theatre in Lafayette, CA. She is the managing editor and blog editor at *Kelp Journal.* She is the former fiction editor at *Please See Me,* the former blog editor at *The Coachella Review,* as well as the former photography editor at *Kelp Journal*. A.M. Larks earned an MFA in creative writing from UC Riverside at Palm Desert, a JD, and a BA in English literature.

Night Swim

by Matt Ellis

Mark emptied his pockets onto the bed before arranging his belongings into an orderly stack on the pillow: cell phone, passport, wallet, and keys. He smoothed his palms over the front and back of his chinos for stray items before pocketing a fold of bills from the nightstand. Satisfied, he tucked the glass jar of his wife's ashes into his leather messenger bag and slid into the hall.

It was late, but he could still hear familiar voices from the patio on the far side of the house, their volume rising with the brass fanfare intro of Jerry Rivera's "Amores Como el Nuestro." Mark had only two options: make a break for the front gate and risk getting trapped in the Panamanian social gravity his sister-in-law Rocio wielded against anyone passing within ten meters of her front patio throne or vault over the back wall into the alley. The latter would put him within the choke-chain slack of the semi-feral beast they'd aptly named Danger, a warning yelled at least a dozen times a day in butchered English to silence the backyard alarm. As numb as Mark felt inside, he'd feel those jaws, and creeping across town with a bleeding backside was problematic. Too many eyes. He'd have to risk a delay.

He passed through the kitchen to peek around the corner into the front room. The voices had ceased, and the TV was turned to the news, a looping traffic-camera feed from Chorrera that showed a chicken-bus cashier hanging out the door until the driver accidentally sideswiped a pole. No trigger warning or censor blot to ready the viewer for the shock. Also, no sight of Rocio. Maybe she slipped off to bed? The front door and five steps to the gate stood between him and freedom. He crossed his fingers, turned the knob, and took a chance.

"Marco! Pa' donde vas?" Rocio called out from the other side of the patio.

Mark wanted to bolt out the gate, but that'd only make her more suspicious. He executed an about-face and saw her slouched in a chair in the corner, her leg kicked over the upholstered arm, beer in hand.

It was here on the patio, during nearly nightly get-togethers, that he'd fallen in love with Mariela. She'd perch on his lap and sing to him, a delicate hand on his neck, everything else melting away. *"Como los unicorns, van desapareciendo. Amar y ser amado, es darse por completo. Un amor como el nuestro—no debe morir jamás.*" He'd felt embarrassed and elated, frozen and timid, unsure how to receive this new love. He'd never wanted it to end.

"Gonna run to the corner," Mark replied in Spanish. "We're low on beer." Mark scanned the corners of the garden and patio for signs of unwanted escorts. Despite the things he'd seen and survived, in places they'd only heard of on the news, things he could never share with them, Rocio would insist on sending someone along. She'd fallen into the role of matriarch since her mother had moved to Massachusetts a few years ago. Rocio still saw Mark as the awkward nineteen-year-old American soldier their baby sister brought home nearly thirty years ago. That wasn't part of his plan. What was in the jar was for the Pacific. Though his body trembled at the thought of releasing this last remnant of Mariela, he'd made a promise. But he'd never promised to share that moment.

"Did the kids get back okay?" Rocio asked.

Mark nodded. The "kids" were in their twenties with lives of their own. One married and on the East Coast, and the other in school out west. But time worked a little differently here. You were frozen in the form they first met you until you'd grown far past it. Nicknames stuck even harder. "They both got home a few hours ago. They send their love."

Rocio nodded before tipping back the bottle and draining it. She clinked the empty down among the others. She stared at him, eyes blinking slowly, a tear forming at the edge. She wasn't much of a drinker. "The service was beautiful…" The dam broke into a steady stream down her cheeks. Judging by the mascara tracks and the bottles, she'd been out here for hours.

Mark left his escape behind, knelt beside her, and kissed her forehead before wiping at the trails of gray. At nearly twenty years her senior, Rocio had been a second mother to Mariela. Mark felt the urge to sit with her and tell stories, but he'd already endured seven nights of this. Watching Mariela's family watching him, as if they heard the music cranking down in his jack-in-the-box mind, bracing themselves for the boom. He needed to find peace. He needed to move on.

"Let's get you to bed," Mark whispered, helping her to her feet.

She patted his hand and floated to the front door but paused. "Grab Javi and Quique to go with you." She craned her neck down the road and pushed out her lips for extra measure. "They're playing dominoes at the basketball court."

Mark nodded. He waited for her to retreat indoors before leaving. He took the long way around the basketball courts, moving from shadow to shadow, not to avoid lurking threats but afraid he might be offered a ride or unwanted company. Aside from his in-laws, he was avoiding people who knew him from before. It was the easiest thing. They were them, but he wasn't him anymore. The only remnant of the young man they knew was his eyes, a blue so deep the porteño women would threaten to steal them away. Mariela had taken his heart instead. Now that was shattered, and his blue eyes were bloodshot. But occasionally, someone would still recognize him. Only because of her—Mariela's gringo.

Gringo wasn't a label to disparage, but to differentiate, always uttered with a smile and an occasional wink. This town had once made him feel special, a foreign concept to a new private on a base where nearly everyone outranked him, requiring snaps to parade rest or sharp, precise salutes. But he wasn't the only one who'd changed. This town, Puerto Armuelles, had followed him down a different branch of the same hard road. It was a stranger now, too, once familiar spaces replaced by imposters and empty shells—a banana boomtown abandoned by the international conglomerates, overcooked by the balmy Central American heat, and pounded by torrential rains. He'd promised to come back often. But, one year rolled into another, excuse layered upon excuse, until the competing reasons and priorities, like him and this town, faded into something unrecognizable. This place had moved on without them. Without her. Why couldn't he?

Mark skirted the main square. It was lit for a Christmas parade the coming week, the palm trees strangled by colorful lights, drawing the local kids and parents like moths. Mark saw a clear path to his final destination, but he needed supplies. He stopped at a corner kiosk to grab a six-pack of Balboa before cutting back over to the Cinta Costera, or, rather, the dirt path where the government had promised a tourist promenade that never materialized. He followed the route to the crumbling Chiriqui Land Company plantain shipping docks, Puerto's most prominent landmark. Beyond this monstrosity was their spot, a slice of beach where, even before they'd bought the land, they'd sneak off and hide below the rocks to explore their new love and young bodies until the rising tides lapped at their feet, sending them scrambling for their clothes and higher ground.

He shotgunned two beers and was halfway through a third when he noticed the mist blowing against him from the crashing tide. He'd always remembered the water being a placid canvas of tiny ripples, drawing and redrawing the moon's stages as their time slipped away. Not tonight. The water roiled as if shocked to life by the lightning storm growing on the horizon.

It was time.

Mark chugged the rest of the six-pack before stripping nude and laying his clothing out on the rocks in tidy Army squares beneath his flip-flops. He didn't question the compulsion. There were no military send-offs without ceremony. Why would this one be any different?

He didn't remember moving from the rocks, but there he stood, naked in the moonlight, the white seafoam lapping at his toes, inviting him to join Mariela again. He walked and then waded. He dove when the waves broke harder, surrendering to the ocean's whim. He wasn't sure what would come next; this was as far as he'd planned. He tried to float, imagining the awaiting moon, stars, and satellites beyond the low ceiling of black clouds. It wasn't long until he was no longer rolling over swells but tossed by crashing waves, smashing him against the sandy bottom until he didn't know his up from down. He tried to succumb, let nature take its course, but his body wouldn't cooperate. Mark's arms and legs flailed for purchase; his lungs, his lips, his tongue struggling for the surface, hungry for air.

A mouthful of foam followed by a long drag against the sand, and he was slammed against a dock beam. He swung his arms out, wrapping them around the old, rotting wood. Another wave tossed him up and away, the barnacles and splintered edges ripping at his forearms and chest, crashing him back down. He bounced from one concrete base to another. He couldn't do this alone. He'd somehow forgotten Mariela in the glass jar on the shore. In a surge of panic, he thrust his feet against the bottom only to find himself waist-deep again and hyperventilating. Another wave toppled him, dragging him across the sand and pebbles before spitting him onto the shore. He'd had a plan, and the water was doing its part. Maybe more. But he needed more courage to finish the journey.

Mark stumbled to his stack of clothes. He felt the sting as he pulled on his pants, the fabric chafing against the abrasions and friction burns from his last bout with the waves. Even in the dark, he saw the shallow rivulets of blood-tinted seawater running down his torso and arms. He laughed at the thought of treating these wounds so near the end, but if someone saw the blood, they'd stop him. They'd ask questions. Try to help. He scooped up a handful of sand and mashed it into the wound on his side, holding it tightly. When he let go, most of the sand fell away, but no more blood trickled out. He did the same with his forearms before slipping his shirt over his head.

Mark could still see the lights in the central square, but everyone had cleared out except for a few vendors still packing their wares. He stumbled to the open window of a food truck.

"We're closed," the woman said in Spanish without turning.

Mark slammed a hundred-dollar bill on the counter, more to keep from falling forward than to grab her attention. She turned.

"Beer," Mark said in Spanish. A hiccup blindsided the rest of his words.

She slid her hand closer to the prize. "I don't sell beer."

"Rum, whiskey, wine, moonshine, gasoline—"

The woman stopped him with her palm before rummaging under the counter. She straightened up and shook a bottle of clear liquid at him, viscous drops hanging tight to the sides before joining the rest. Mark squinted to read the label, both sun-bleached and oil-stained—indecipherable. She sniffed it and grimaced before handing it out to him. "That's all I got."

Mark pulled at the bottle, but the woman's grip held. She tugged it back, tipping him off-balance. "I don't have change."

"Keep it," Mark said, and she let go. He took a heavy pull and nearly spit it out. Maybe she was calling his bluff about the gasoline. No. It was alcohol, alright, but was it the drinking kind? The burn plummeted to his stomach, and a volcano of fumes rushed back up, forcing out a puff of surrender. He could already feel his head swimming in choppier waters. He pulled out the rest of his cash, now just a damp clump of bills, and tossed it on the counter. He wouldn't need it. Before he could turn, the woman whistled and thrust a Styrofoam container at him. Mark swayed and shook his head.

"Please," she said. "I insist." Mark snatched the container and swung back toward his beach. He could hear the woman battening down her kitchen and speeding off, probably worried he'd come to his senses and ask for change. He hadn't thought this clearly in years.

By the time Mark reached his beach, the distant storm had blown farther north up the Pacific, and the light from the full moon had broken through the clouds and onto the sand. He'd taken several more swigs from the mystery bottle and was fatigued from his first attempt at good-bye. He sat down on an outcropping of rocks and opened the container. It was stuffed with fried pork. He grabbed a piece and sniffed at it; the sweet smell turned his stomach. He laughed at the thought of Mariela yelling after the children to wait thirty minutes after eating before swimming—they'd get cramps. And then he cried again, his sobs turning into deep moans and then to whimpers. But the whimpers weren't his. He looked to his left and saw a stray dog, nothing but bones and mangy fur.

He shook the container at the dog and set it on the ground. Mark stared at the mongrel, who sniffed and then devoured his gift. "If you'll excuse me," Mark said, tipping the bottle to his new friend of convenience and taking his final pull. If he waited any longer, he wouldn't complete his journey. Not tonight. So he stripped off his shirt and opened the jar, stuffing his wife's ashes in his pants pockets until the jar was empty. He took baby steps into the ocean this time, the surface as calm as he'd always remembered—to his ankles, calves, and then his waist. The light from the moon glimmered across the now shallow waves, illuminating the surface as Mariela's ashes expanded out from Mark's pockets in a halo, carrying her off to a peaceful rest to wait for his turn. When the cloudy water cleared, he continued to sink to his stomach and chest. Then Mark heard someone calling out in Spanish, "Aren't you scared of sharks?"

Mark turned and squinted into the dark. The silhouette of a man had joined the feasting dog.

"There are no sharks," Mark replied in Spanish.

"Do you doubt their existence or just out here?" the voice yelled. Mark glanced from side to side, his certainty waning. He squinted at the moonlit water, but there were too many pockets of darkness where the waves crested, shadows playing near the surface. Was it flotsam or fins? Driftwood? He felt something brush his ankle. Seaweed? He braced himself, imagined clamping jaws, the invisible threat dragging his thrashing body out to sea. Before he realized it, he was running back to shore, his knees pumping high. He slowed as he reached the interloper— a wild, gaping smile greeted him from a mouth that had seen its fair share of mutiny. The man was slight—sun-kilned leather skin pulled taut over sinewy muscle and a face of hard lines. His age was a mystery.

"You run pretty fast for a man who doesn't believe in sharks," the old man said.

"I just forgot to take off my pants," Mark said. "Too hard to swim."

The old man scoffed. "Your pants are the only reason I came over this time."

"Pardon me if I made you uncomfortable."

"On the contrary, I wanted to give you privacy." The old man gestured to Mark's waist. "The water can get pretty cold." The old man waited for the joke to land. When it didn't, he accentuated it with a slap to Mark's shoulder. "Less for the sharks to clamp onto, you know what I mean?"

Mark cast an angry arm out at the ocean. "There are no sharks out there."

"My friend, there are sharks everywhere. I'm a shark"— the old man pointed at himself, then at the dog—"He's a shark, for sure. Are you telling me you're not a shark?"

Mark unbuttoned his pants. He hadn't wanted an audience for this last performance but wouldn't stop the show.

"Wait," the old man said, holding up an aging flip phone. "Could you take a picture of my wife and me?"

Mark looked past him and noticed a ramshackle beach cottage adjacent to his plot of land. Somehow, he'd never noticed it before, but it was impossible to miss now, lit with fat Christmas lightbulbs. A gaudy yellow star the size of a compact car was on the roof. A woman waved timidly from her hiding spot behind the half-opened front door. Blood rushed to Mark's face, and he scrambled for his shirt. "Apologies."

The old man cackled until he coughed. "You think you're the first gringo to skinny-dip here? Last week, we had some German lady strip down right in front of our house." With his hands, the old man drew curvy lines in the air, a whistle crescendo accentuating the invisible hips. "Now that was a show."

Mark wanted to laugh, but more so, he wanted his privacy.

"Honestly," the old man said, "you're lucky you got me and not my gringo neighbor." The old man leaned in close, his hand cupped to mask his words from imagined eavesdroppers. "I've never met the guy, but I've heard he's quite an asshole."

Mark grabbed the flip phone and gestured toward the house. Maybe compliance was the best option for shooing this pest away. The old man stood by the house and beckoned his wife forward. Mark nodded and waved for them to move closer together, trying to fit them and their house into the tiny flip phone viewfinder. He tapped the button. It should never have worked—the darkness between Mark and the couple, the bright colored lights behind. But it was beautiful. Mark felt a rush of emotions not crashing down on his shoulders but coursing through his veins. He thought of mornings with his granddaughter and her first Christmas tree. He'd play acoustic guitar while she beat out her sounds on the spruce top, goo-gooing her vocals. The images of other Christmases flashed before him, hoisting his kids high up on his shoulders to place the star on the tree top until they were too big to lift anymore. He hadn't repeated that tradition with his granddaughter yet. He never would.

"Hey!" The old man walked forward. "Care to share?"

Mark smiled and handed the phone to the old man, a strange pang of pride swelling inside. Was it from the picture? This strange moment? When was the last time he'd felt this?

"Not bad," the old man said. He beamed with joy and showed it to his wife. "Not bad at all."

Mark was frozen, unsure of what to do next. The old man gestured to the open door. "How about a drink?"

Mark looked down at his feet, sand-caked, seawater still dripping from his pants. "I think I'd better—"

"Tomorrow, then," the old man said. "You watch fut?"

"Not really. But I won't be able to—"

"Good! World Cup finals are tomorrow. We're making lechon and tamales. Bring a dessert and some beer. And not any of that flavored gringo shit. Regular beer. National beer." With that, the old man disappeared into the house.

"I'm sorry," the woman said. "He's a handful when he's drinking."

"It's okay, señora," Mark said. "None of this is what I wanted, but it was exactly what I needed."

The woman bent forward, held Mark's bicep, and gently kissed him on the cheek. "Then we'll see you tomorrow?" Her eyes moved along his arm to the tattoo on his forearm—a military dagger crossed with a fountain pen. "You seem like the punctual type. Let's make it two." With a wink, she left Mark to consider the appropriate pastry for the people who had saved his life.

Matt Ellis is a slow-traveling freelance writer and photographer whose work has been featured in *The Insider*, *Publishers Weekly*, *Kirkus*, the *Los Angeles Review of Books*, *Canvas Rebel*, and *Pseudopod*.

Queen of the Metas

By Hannah Knighton

"A good amount of the job is observational," Taylor Sakmar said as he crouched in front of a tank, peering in at the unusual, multicolored creature staring back at him. It was early September and my first day as a cephalopod operations intern at the Marine Biological Laboratory (MBL) in Woods Hole, Massachusetts. Sakmar stood to step aside so I could begin to make some observations of my own.

Looking back at me through a W-shaped pupil was a *Metasepia pfefferi,* commonly known as the flamboyant cuttlefish, a name inspired by its vibrant color palette, with eight arms ranging from shades of pink and yellow to orange and brown waving gently with the flow of the water. Its mantle, the main body cavity, flashed bands of brown and white. Like a cool breeze pricks goosebumps across human skin, soft tissue known as papillae mocked horns all over the creature's body as it bobbed close to the water surface.

"With these guys, it's actually not a good sign to see them swimming around. It usually means they're stressed," Sakmar said. *Metasepia pfefferi,* often referred to in the lab simply as metas, are the smallest species of cuttlefish, at their largest growing to about the size of a credit card. They spend much of their time on the ground, trudging slowly across the sand and nestling under rocks or shells. Sakmar, the senior cephalopod culture specialist at MBL, relayed a list of other behaviors to look out for and left me to begin distributing snacks of live grass shrimp to the colorful creatures.

From then on, I would be the point woman for this species (Queen of the Metas, as one co-worker jokes). Everything from feedings to cleaning the intake tubes that supplied water to their tanks would fall under the umbrella of my responsibility. But my ultimate goal was to "close the life cycle"—in other words, get them to reproduce. Successful reproduction and subsequent maintenance of ideal growth conditions are referred to as culturing. The cephalopod lab aims to culture a variety of species as we work to define and maintain the standard of care for cephalopods in lab and aquarium settings.

Being crowned Queen of the Metas was not a title to take lightly. Nicknamed the divas of the sea, these cuttlefish are easily stressed and difficult to care for in captivity. In fact, my supervisor, Bret Grasse, was the first to successfully have this species lay eggs and raise those hatchlings to adulthood in captivity at the Monterey Bay Aquarium in California in 2010.

Cephalopods, the class that includes squid, octopus, and the chambered nautilus alongside cuttlefish, are sensitive creatures, generally easily stressed. That means even obtaining the species and acclimating them to human care was difficult. From there, the challenges only continued.

Prior to Grasse's work in culturing the flamboyant cuttlefish, very little was known about the species. The only notes that existed were from divers or researchers observing the cuttlefish in their natural habitat in the Indo-Pacific—there was no knowledge of keeping them in lab or aquarium settings. He figured out what prey items they preferred, what kind of substrate and rock formations they liked, and where they preferred to lay eggs. But once they lay eggs, that's where the real challenge starts.

They have to hatch away from any adults or aggressive flow so they can begin the early, most sensitive stages of their lives in the most optimal conditions possible. The first time these optimal conditions were obtained and baby *Metasepia* began to hatch, Grasse felt a large sense of relief. He believes this pioneer work paved the way for a deeper scientific understanding of cephalopods. Since then, they've become integral in aquariums worldwide and are now being investigated as model organisms for human disease research.

Today, the cephalopod operations team works to produce multiple generations of various cephalopod species with the goal of raising organisms for aquariums or for human disease modeling, such as anesthetic testing, limb regeneration studies, and genetic testing. Captive culturing programs like ours help to reduce the strain on wild populations and maintain nature's biodiverse habitats, making this practice sustainable.

Sakmar wasn't kidding when he said most of the job was observational. I would spend the next month trying to determine each cuttlefish's gender from simply watching their behavior. Flamboyant cuttlefish show little sexual dimorphism, meaning there are no physical external characteristics to determine their gender. The only physical characteristic to look for is size, as females tend to get slightly bigger. But that can be a tricky and not always reliable way to distinguish them. Instead, the way they act unveils their sex.

One day I hopped up on a step stool to drop a few shrimps into a tank at feeding time. I came eye level with two metas having a face-off. Both metas had their arms outstretched; they were light in color except the tips of their arms, which had turned to black. They wiggled back and forth, dusting each other with their outstretched arms. I watched for a moment before turning and calling out to Sakmar. He walked over to where I was standing with my eyes glued to the tank. "That's what we call paint brushing."

As I had observed it, paint brushing is a form of male-versus-male aggression. The more dominant male, which in this case was the larger male, wins. Males will also exhibit this behavior when mating to determine if a fellow flamboyant is male or female. As I had learned, males will return aggression, while females will be submissive, usually a sign they're willing to mate. But other times, as I often observed, the females simply try to get away.

Cephalopods, sometimes referred to as the shape-shifters of the sea, are able to create dazzling color displays and achieve a range of body patterning by manipulating a combination of factors. Behind their ability to create such displays is an important group of cells known as chromatophores. Chromatophores are pigment-containing cells that have muscles attached to them. Imagine how spokes look on a bicycle—that's how the muscles surround these sacs of pigment. The muscles expand and contract the cells, allowing for the variety of colors a cephalopod can put on display. Body postures, like the one termed paint brushing, can also be made up of textural components, when papillae extend outward to form small, soft peaks on the animal.

There are other behaviors aside from paint brushing that help aquarists determine the gender of metas. Males, for example, typically seek higher ground, while females will spend more time under rocks and shells. But metas rarely make things easy, and their tricky tactics can only add to the confusion. Some males will be more submissive, making them appear to be females to caretakers. In other populations there may be dominant females that display male behaviors.

As they get older and closer to sexual maturity, the act is eventually dropped, and distinguishing sex differences comes easily. While males still react slowly and feed meticulously, female *Metasepia* begin to take out shrimp with gusto. Females quickly lock their W-shaped pupils with their prey and aim their feeding tentacles with great accuracy. Previously eating one shrimp per meal, they'll now take down three to five times more food as they put vast amounts of energy into ova production. Metas are often slow-moving creatures, so when they begin to eagerly attack prey, it's a good sign for reproductive health. As the days passed, I noticed the metas were getting hungrier, the females were getting larger, and the males were paint brushing more and more. We had to be close to getting eggs, I was sure of it.

While cleaning a tank on an afternoon at the end of October, I noticed a small, white blob bouncing along the sand. Eyes widened and heart racing, I began to look under rocks and shells. Sure enough, on the underside of one large scallop shell clung seven small sacs of tissue. Eggs. EGGS. We had eggs! I clambered around the lab excitedly looking for Sakmar. "We have eggs!" Sakmar did a spin, punched the air excitedly, and shouted, "Yes!"

* * *

From the end of October through December, I practiced techniques in harvesting and incubating *Metasepia* eggs. Carefully lifting low-hanging rocks and checking under the smooth, vaulted surfaces of shells, I'd find clutches of around a dozen eggs delicately waving with the undulations of the water in the tank. When females are ready to lay their eggs, they seek out low, vaulted surfaces. Lifting their arms up into shells or low-hanging rocks, they carefully deposit eggs one by one, tacking them to the chosen surface with a biological glue.

Taking sharp-tipped forceps, I gently scraped away the biological adhesive connecting the eggs to the shells, delicately plucking them off and carefully depositing them into a bucket of seawater, one by one. The importance of the task was not lost on me. Every dime-sized egg felt valuable, a small promise of life within. Every step I took during harvesting could affect the possibility of that small promise reaching reality. Although just an intern, I felt I had been given a great task, and with it, the inherent pressure of succeeding in nurturing each little life.

At the MBL, our mission is to work toward creating and providing the standard of care for cephalopod species. This includes optimizing the animals' hatching success, which is why we practice techniques in artificial incubation. Artificial incubation, as opposed to keeping the eggs in the tank with their mothers and other co-habituating adults, allows for close observation and proper oxygenation of embryos. Cuttlefish mothers provide little to no maternal care, and removing eggs from their habitat allows the females to lay additional viable eggs. This method is also safer for hatchlings who may find their parent's environment harsh with high water flow that could push them around and the possibility of being mistaken for prey by adults. In the end, artificial incubation allows aquarists and researchers to create the most optimal conditions for hatching.

As the days passed and the embryos bounced and bubbled around inside their incubators, the transparency of the egg casing welcomed me into their tiny worlds. I watched as their beady, red eyespots developed, their heads and arms began to form and wrap around the yolk. Their mantles began protruding, followed by the formation of chromatophores, the pigment cells that allow for their color-changing abilities. Right before my own eyes, I watched tiny replicates of adult *Metasepia* form. I began to feel attached to the growing embryos, as if I had laid the eggs myself.

By January, hatchlings had taken over the lab. Still leading the care of the adults and now their 220 offspring, I would dote on the tiny cuttlefish, carefully conducting counts each morning, then feeding them. Feeding would take an hour and a half of my morning or longer, as I meticulously assessed the number of miniature mysid shrimp to place into the tank. Mindful not to startle them, I would bend down and peer into the tank with an angled flashlight to watch them feed. Their tiny movements were minuscule. They'd turn slowly, bounding around on mantle papillac projections known as glutapods, a term that quite literally means "butt feet."

Over countless hours of feeding and caring for these delicate animals, I created my own narrative with the critters. I'd chide the chunky ones for taking more food than their fair share, although regardless, I was happy to see them eating and growing, as any caretaker would be. Just like a litter of puppies, there tended to be a runt in each group. I'd keep a close eye on the little guys during feeding to make sure they got at least one shrimp each. Time consuming as it was, it was time that never felt wasted. The early stages of life are the most critical.

As I astutely cared for the delicate divas, a new idea was forming. I had now spent every day for around five months observing and caring for these creatures. The pressure to succeed in raising the cuttlefish kept me working at my highest caliber. I felt my understanding of their care was not quite perfected, but reached a professional level. My notes had begun to pile up, my observations numerous. I wanted to dig deeper; there was much to still be discovered about these animals beyond their care and keeping.

*　*　*

It was summertime, and Woods Hole had evolved into a different town. Once quaint and quiet, it had transformed into a bustling beachside hot spot. I often describe the change from the winter to the summer as a human migration. Thousands of people flock to the Cape; everyone from vacationers to summer researchers fill up the campus and bring a whole new life to the area.

There was a new breath of life for my work at MBL, too. As I harvested and incubated the transparent orbs of life, I was welcomed into their tiny world, watching them hit developmental milestones safe inside their eggs, yet right before my eyes. Despite all the ongoing and already published research about cephalopod embryonic development, I found the literature lacking for *Metasepia*. So, I made a plan and typed up an experiment proposal. Grasse and Sakmar approved, agreeing the existing information felt incomplete. Just as I had fostered the growth of the cuttlefish themselves, I would now be nurturing my own research project.

My experiment aimed to look at and mark the growth of *Metasepia*. As days passed, I would note at what point in gestation key anatomical features began to form. With a delicate hand, I'd manipulate the position of the growing *Metasepia* under the microscope, trying to get the best angle for an image. I photographed them in this manner three times a week, and I did it for three weeks, watching as they developed key morphological features such as eyes, arms, cuttlebones, and chromatophores.

Through the clear outer egg casing at the yolk, I saw the first sign of organ development, which are two dark, half-moon-shaped spots forming on the yolk's surface. These half-moons will quickly form into eyestalks, and a central protrusion from the yolk becomes the cuttlefish's main body cavity, the mantle. Below are eight dots that will soon develop into arms. As the arms develop, they wrap around the yolk such that the animal appears to be grasping its source of sustenance. The animal grows and the yolk shrinks, and a distinct head forms. The arms and the mantle elongate, and after twenty days, the cuttle-bone—the internal hard structure that aids in buoyancy control—and the color-shifting chromatophores have formed. The animal inside the egg is a tiny replica of an adult flamboyant cuttlefish, fully equipped with all its body parts, even able to camouflage and dispense ink inside its egg sac.

The *Metasepia* took about twenty-nine days to hatch. The imaging process went by quickly, and before we knew it, tanks throughout the lab were once again populated with the tiny creatures bounding around on their glutapods and flashing their vibrant bands of color. My focus could now turn to data analysis.

After running through the records and looking for significant milestones, I found the embryos developed consistently, with only one individual lagging behind. I was able to mark at what day, over weeks of development, key anatomical features could be expected to develop. These initial insights are a prerequisite to further understanding of the development and evolution of *Metasepia,* which in turn allows aquarists and researchers to track normal growth in captive-held metas. A world of scientists and aquarists could potentially benefit from this.

It could even have the potential for publication. For me, this was the ultimate validation of the trials and triumphs I had experienced over my time with the cephalopod program.

I realized that despite the fact I had been mentored almost exclusively by male faculty members, it was my own attention to detail and nurturing qualities, which one might label "feminine," that had led to my success. I often found myself doubting my own intrinsic abilities, but those inherent qualities were ultimately the key to my success. On the last day of my internship at MBL, I sat down with another great mind, Dr. Carrie Albertin, an embryologist known for her work sequencing the genome of the California two-spot octopus. Grasse believed Albertin would provide expert guidance as I contemplated going through with the publication process. As I sat in her office, I found myself apologizing for my research, stating it wasn't quite on the level of what she does, but it could still have value to researchers. Albertin stopped me in my tracks. "What you've done here is real research. And there's no doubt you can publish this. I would be happy to look at it for you and point you in the best direction I can."

As two women sitting across from each other, I felt she must have a depth of understanding to my doubts one could only sympathize with through their own similar experiences. My gratitude for her confidence in me was an overwhelming feeling, possibly as overwhelming as the amount of thank-yous that poured out of me as we talked. "Go be excellent," Albertin said as I left her office. Washed over with emotion, I turned and smiled back; I finally saw I have what it takes to be a scientist. I don't need to fulfill a male-dominated "scientist" archetype; I just need to follow my sense of curiosity and practice skills of discipline and observation, qualities that were always within me.

Hannah Knighton is a freelance writer and editor with focuses on wildlife, environment, sustainability, and travel topics. Her work has been published with *Smithsonian Magazine* online, the Ocean Portal, and *Motif Magazine* and her editorial contributions extend to *Science Magazine*, *Science News* online, and *the Science Writer*. She holds dual bachelor's degrees in marine science and English from Jacksonville University and a master's degree in science writing from Johns Hopkins University. More recently, she began exploring themes of grief, race, identity, and motherhood through her essays. Her writing reflects a profound connection between the intricacies of the natural world and the human experience.

Conversations with Birds
by Priyanka Kumar

Review by A.M. Larks

In *Conversations with Birds,* writer and filmmaker Priyanka Kumar introduces the reader to not only the world of birding but the why of birding and its natural progression into a naturalist mindset through her own journey and encounters in the wild.

Loosely structuring the book around encounters with specific bird species like tanagers, cranes, goshawks, and bald eagles, Kumar relates more than her experience observing these creatures. In each essay, Kumar not only introduces us to the gifts of the natural world and the awe of experiencing it, but also the constant and undeniable peril it is in.

Kumar's writing is vivid, poetic, and devasting. Birds are the guiding light by which Kumar is able to engage in the landscape, but her background as a storyteller allows her to see beyond the constraints of birding life lists (lists of birds to see before one dies) and into the larger world and our place in it. Or rather, more aptly, what we have done to it.

Creating refuges, while helpful, as a stopgap measure to declining animal populations do not stem the tide if habitat needs and food sources are not also protected. Kumar draws attention to these myopic efforts like saving only the nesting tree of a predator bird but clear-cutting the rest of its forest territory. All of which render the conservation effort essentially moot. Kumar's boots-on-the-ground observations of animals that appear further back on the evolutionary timeline than we do, make the reader wonder who is entitled to possession of this valuable real estate we call Earth. Are humans, in fact, the trespassers?

Kumar's answer to the ethics of how we live is to talk about sustainability and to reevaluate our standards. Shouldn't other species, like birds, be more than just not extinct? Shouldn't they be numerous? Thriving, not only surviving?

Through birding and her various adventures to see, experience, and understand the world that we all live in and on, Kumar seamlessly braids together wonder, curiosity, travesty, and hope. "There is no magic herb that can heal the wounds caused by the inexorable march of industrialization. What remains in our power, however, is to alter how we see the natural world and to appreciate that this finely tuned biome (what's left of it) sustains numberless creatures, including us."

A.M. Larks's writing has appeared in *NiftyLit, Scoundrel Time, Assay: A Journal of Nonfiction Studies, Five on the Fifth, Charge Magazine*, and he *ZYZZYVA* and *Ploughshares* blogs. She has served as a judge for the Loud Karma Productions' Emerging Female and Nonbinary Playwriting Award and has performed her stories at Lit Up at Town Hall Theatre in Lafayette, CA. She is the managing editor and blog editor at *Kelp Journal*. She is the former fiction editor at *Please See Me*, the former blog editor at *The Coachella Review*, as well as the former photography editor at *Kelp Journal*. A.M. Larks earned an MFA in creative writing from UC Riverside at Palm Desert, a JD, and a BA in English literature.

lawrencetown beach
(mostly frozen summer surf)

even with the suit
legs freezing in
      summer waters while
      rocks wound and
      edge feet cut to bits
and red faced and
a half
hearted paddle out
(and a day of one of
those one of those days)
the paddle out
and sloppy ways and
      sloppy waves and fighting
      the rip played out arms creased
      nothing right not rightly for a left
      and mushy waves white foam and
      last nights wind never came down
(and you know)
that gut feeling cold and balled up
you know in that deep blue
      that deep blue part
      waves in carpets and kegs
      carpets and kegs rolling in

                        you know something's
                        something watching you
                        under somewhere and it's
time time to call
last ride and
ride the next wave
all the wave in
way in

it's the locals
you can't see
that just may have teeth
and tempers to match

makapu'u first day waves

got off a plane two days before
drove out
first waves
smiling and nothing
can break through
            at the top
                    and the water rising
                            the wave jacks up
                                pushing sliding
                                    and the board too
                                sliding and gravity bent bends

                    and free energy
                 and caught it so surprised
              and never made
forgot the bottom turn

stupid smiles perma grinning
never made it just
               straight down blue blur
               in white foam and
               a tube roar behind me
               straight in beach side
rode til the
shore hit
board bottom
beached and dug in
couldn't say a thing
that's the smile
they're all talking
about

kunduchi beach long ago now

often
thinking
about the
very length
so much sand
water blue and
a little under the
weather always so
very nice and the smile
feet so hot on the white
sand underneath and the
cooler is there before you
can say no and you don't want
to not really for its hot and a drink
could be cool and loquacious running
down kunduchi for a long time a stretch
its true so long ago i remember such a time
and some rock and corals also there to stub toes
and a blue boat and a black man and white teeth with
rope around his shorts and a basket balanced in vertigo
but not as bad as spinning of course more to the sway and
the swaying palms and softy ice cream winds onshore
cooling

and worried about the car and the vinyl heats the smell of
plastic
sand dancing from seat to seat and just a check and a dry
towel and
no need no want no idea to be in that car so near the beach
and that real
good day of days after the trip out of the city kind of like
the light from california
but not and much more to it than all that and a lilt of the
radios and the kids run up
and down the sands so going on and on and on and the
day lasting almost as long
there's a point of end in the distance but around a bend
and another side and going on
long walks good for my head so thinking it could be so
but kunduchi always is and the
same sensitivity and warm winds protect me the same as
long ago i sit and thinking
about what then

Mike Sluchinski is a mature part-time University of
Saskatchewan student and does construction and
demolition work. He often listens to his Thai astrologer
and his wife, although rarely in that order. Blessed and
favored by faith, he prays every day, especially short ones,

sometimes under his breath if there's hammers and nails involved. His poetry has been published in *Freefall* , *In Media Res*, and *Grain* magazines.

An Excerpt from CASCADIA
- a novel

by Art Hanlon

I still have, somewhere, the famous photo that appeared on the front page of the *Berkeley Barb*, the one that caught me standing atop a burned-out police car at the People's Park fiasco in 1969, power chording my field guitar, a twenty-dollar thrift store Stella, with its painfully high action and its floating bridge and rattling metal tailpiece. I played the buzzing tailpiece as if it were feedback—acoustic analog feedback. That was my moment caught on film, the public record. *Time* magazine even picked it up, although I wasn't identified in the cutline. I was high on my fifteen minutes, standing on that scorched black-and-white chassis, singing antiwar songs in a top hat and a faded-green Marine Corps battle jacket. Caterina, *la Pasionaria*, the daughter of Dust Bowl radicals, my red-diaper-baby girlfriend in an Apache headband, her brown braids flying, climbed up to stand right next to me to sing out the harmonies with her fist clenched and raised as I chorded the machine that kills fascists: *¡No pasarán!* Very inspiring, not to mention suicidal. *Showtime!* the billboard sign said atop the arched façade of the Forum Restaurant. Catie and I would have made a great poster for the siege of Madrid, winning the battles but losing the proxy war. And sure enough, a few minutes later, the Alameda County Sheriff's Department entered the scene, oversized, red-faced Southern boys imported from Georgia who thought they were fighting the Vietcong, bursting out of Sproul Plaza, encased in blue jumpers with their tear gas, nightsticks, and Mossbergs loaded with double-aught buck.

Yeah. That was my private Suribachi, six years after my release from the Marines. Henckel had been long gone to the East Coast, disappointed because he wanted me to go with him. Except I had found Caterina, my mission, and my tribe, and so I made my stand, and some would say on the wrong side because the rout only took a half an hour that day, or even less. Time gets weird in situations like that. Most everyone fled straight down Telegraph toward Oakland in this huge running mass. My fucking tribe, all assholes and elbows, running on patchouli fumes, rage and fear, inhabiting a crazed borderline, the outer fringe of nonviolence, unarmed on purpose, the zone where martyrs and angels live. Our eyes were burning from tear gas, but Caterina and I rushed across Telegraph to get to Dwight, tripping over the metal newspaper boxes that had been thrown into the littered street, paper scraps and dust filling the air, hopping over students and street hippies rolling on the pavement while the Alameda County Sheriff's Department grimly swung those nightsticks. The Caffe Mediterraneum was trashed; Moe's Books had wisely closed down, but the clerks in Shakespeare and Company on the corner of Dwight stood in the doorway with handkerchiefs pressed to their faces, watching the scene unfold. It was crazy confusing, paper scraps scattered all over the avenue, tear gas canisters spewing burning toxic white clouds, the display blankets of the street vendors whipping down Telegraph, their beads and jewelry scattered like broken glass across the sidewalk, a small-scale Kristallnacht, a warning shot of sorts that echoed eventually all the way to Kent State, Jackson State University, and beyond.

I grabbed Catie's arm as she landed on her feet already running, my guitar at sling arms, and we cut up Dwight to Dynamite Annie's apartment on Regent Street. Once there, we felt giddy at first, now that we were safe in the company of a roomful of musicians and students, fellow travelers nervously passing joints around, all caught up in the momentous drama of the day. When the helicopters came close, a young woman in the kitchen began crying; then the flurry of hollow popping sounds down on Telegraph shut everyone up.

"What was that?" someone asked. I knew it was gunfire and told everyone to stay in the apartment without telling them why. Bad time for anyone to be running through the streets to get home. Some of us with wet kerchiefs covering mouth and nose took turns rinsing the tear gas out of eyes and hair at the kitchen sink. Strange, but I remember marking the moment as I watched Caterina wash her face, couldn't take my eyes off her. She was flushed with righteous fervor, tossing her braids back over her shoulders before scooping up water to her face. She ignored her reflection in the jagged glass fragment of a broken mirror propped against the exposed water pipes over the sink, so she didn't see what I saw: the battle light shining through her face, eyes glowing with excited fulfillment as she smiled to herself, the red Buddhist prayer strings threading a few glass beads through her brown braids. She was so eager for the next thing, whatever it would be, and I ached with love as I had a fleeting but intense moment completely absorbed in her complicated, seemingly out-of-my-range allure and the possibility of a more or less permanent *us* rising above even the strange post-battle euphoria we all felt. I had it all at that moment: righteous action for a righteous cause, honor, a girlfriend to share the moment. We actually thought we were winning, until later that evening when we got the news that the bastards had killed James Rector and blinded Alan Blanchard. Yeah. I remember their names. Don't you? We all crashed pretty thoroughly then, and the euphoria gave way to a wary seriousness when we realized what we were really up against. Later, Catie wept with bitter anger when she heard what Governor Reagan had to say: "If it takes a bloodbath, let's get it over with."

It feels like light years since I last saw Catarina alive. A minor rollerblading accident while visiting our Buddhist friends in Boulder, Colorado. An aneurysm after swerving out of control and hitting her head on the stone wall lining the path in a Canyon Boulevard park. She got right up after she crashed. She was wearing a helmet, and although she hit the wall pretty hard, embarrassment seemed to be the chief consequence. That night, she complained of a headache, and the next day she collapsed. Six months after the funeral, an Oakland hills firestorm destroyed the house we had been renting in Berkeley. I got back from Brennan's late and stood in the street at 2:00 a.m., surrounded by fire trucks, police cars, hoses, and neighbors watching it all go. Margo from across the street, whose house had not been touched by the flames, came over to console me, her arm around my shoulder. "First your wife," she said. "And now this. Poor baby."

Poor, well-intentioned Margo. Confused because I was laughing while I wiped away tears. For the first time since the funeral, I was actually happy. Yes, happy. Exhilarated, even. What's that old haiku by Masahide? *Barn's burned down; now I can see the moon?* Oh yes, I hated myself for it, believe me. Change is good, the fatuous ones say. But some changes come too fast and too hard, even when you expect them. The subsequent emotional crash was inevitable, so I was grateful when Josh, an old friend from journalism school who had become the managing editor of the Pacific Slope News Service, mercy hired me. He told me to get out of town and work for a while on the *Pacific Coaster,* one of their alternate weekly newspapers near Seattle, up among the rhodies, the cedars, the Doug firs, the fearless chickaree squirrels. I hated giving up my plan to buy a house in Berkeley, but I had been freelancing too long, and the cost of housing had gotten way ahead of me. The money just wasn't there to keep me in Berkeley, so I moved the little I had left up to the dream they call *Cascadia* and rented a house on an island. After enough time, I suppose a dream deferred becomes a dream abandoned. *Vector Zero.*

And today? Well, I still make the rounds at a few of the bars downtown. I'm finally at the point in my life where I'm pretty much settled in as a part-time local musician and part-time guitar teacher with a not quite full-time day job as a *quiet* newspaper man, a recorder of small, inconsequential stories trying to draw sly amusement out of the police blotter for the alternative weeklies strung out in university towns across America. Still do the tai chi thing, still big on the walking meditation. My early *martial* years? Dead and buried, as far as I was concerned, irrelevant to the major part of my career as a human.

The bluish morning light was coming up, and as it did so, I remembered something deep in my pile of saved possessions, almost forgotten. I went into the garage and squeezed my way through a few questionable objet d'art mechanical devices—all that had survived the Oakland fire. There wasn't much: an antique samovar from a Russian émigré's estate sale, a rock tumbler, extra tables— oak, Formica, metal, glass—stacks of cardboard boxes packed with books still smelling of smoke, photo albums, three or four kerosene lanterns, an old brass bed. I crawled through the clutter of the past all the way to the blank, unpainted Sheetrock of the back wall, where I found hanging from a hook my dust-covered road-trip rucksack from my pre-Catie wandering days, a threadbare God's eye tucked into a crease in the top pocket lid. It was a military-type rucksack with an aluminum frame ancient enough to be held together by buckles instead of Velcro. Behind the backpack, I finally grasped what I had been looking for: the strap of a beaded leather, Northern Cheyenne possibles bag originally belonging to my US cavalryman great-grandfather, one of the so-called Custer's Avengers. The bag contained my Marine memorabilia. The strap was looped around a Mt. Fuji walking staff I had purchased for a hundred yen in Gotemba, Japan, as I prepared to climb Mt. Fuji. I don't know how I got to Gotemba from the hospital in Yokosuka. I was stoned on prescription drugs and Suntory.

The possibles bag slid down into my hands when I removed the staff from the brackets on the wall, still smelling of smoke from the house fire. I brought the walking staff, the God's eye, and the possibles bag into the house and arranged them on the dining room table.

The sun, full of promise, was almost up, its inquisitive light beginning to spill over the Cascades. The dark green leaves of the rhodies were beaded with dew. I heard the ghostly barking of a formation of geese cruising the migratory interstate just overhead, dipping close to the house, close to the earth. I put the diamond-shaped God's eye on the top flap of the possibles bag, and suddenly breathless, I had to sit, my heart rising in my throat so fast

I almost couldn't choke it down. Maybe this wasn't such a good idea.

Catie had made the God's eye for my birthday when we were living in a farmhand's shack on a dairy farm on the Eel River floodplain in Humboldt County. I held the God's eye by one of the two thin branches from a California madrone she'd used for the cruciate armature. She had used black yarn to weave the inner diamond and red and yellow yarn to weave the outside and interior borders.

At the time, Catie was taking classes at Humboldt State University, and we read and studied at night by lamplight to the sound of moths tapping on the lampshade, amid the smell of dust, hay, cattle, and grass on the wind, and listened to string quartets, amused at how the music harmonized with the chorus of peepers and crickets outside. I worked long days in the newsroom at the *Eureka-Arcata Journal* and would come home to find Catie reading on the porch in thick, late-afternoon sunlight amid the tinkling of the bells hanging from the necks of the milk cows grazing in the field across the road. She had a way of folding her legs up under her on the porch swing, graceful as a long-legged water bird, her Flavian curls careening in spiraling meanders, flanking her olive cheeks, framing her troubled eyes, the haunted image in a Pompeii mural. I would get my guitar and she her dulcimer or the autoharp, and we would play and sing, adjusting our pitch in harmony with the faint gravel-throated hum of tractors working the fields, a droning *tractori continuo* we called it, the Doppler shifts in pitch our chief challenge, the aural inspiration for the Dust Bowl suite we were composing.

Most of the time, Catie and I were happy, a state of being at odds with the condition of the world. We were at peace with each other, living on faith alone that the living-in-a-floodplain-shack period of our lives would give way to something more. A fool's paradise, as it turned out, but at least it was possible for a brief time to actually believe something along those lines. We weren't alone in that. I don't know about the others, but I know I'll never again see the world in such a hopeful way. It's hard to believe anymore that any human being ever will. See, even then, even when it seemed like we were winning, we still didn't know what we were up against.

Catie! Catie! Catie! I stood up in a sudden fit of red anger, ready to destroy everything in sight. I mean to tell you I was ready for major mayhem, on the edge of going downtown and getting blind drunk and doing violence to some luckless asshole in the wrong dive bar who said the wrong fucking thing at the wrong time, but…goddammit, there was nothing to be angry about, unless it was time's arrow, and what could be more irrational than that? It was so tempting to give in to that other deeper abyss behind the anger—the hot little chamber where murder lives. It would all be settled then. A bad end. Or maybe a good end. I don't know. Suicide by cop. I'd heard of it.

www.ingramcontent.com/pod-product-compliance
Lightning Source LLC
Chambersburg PA
CBHW040908010826
48978CB00013BB/1199